James Butler

Fortune's Foot-Ball

Or, the adventures of Mercutio: founded on matters of fact. A novel. Part 1

James Butler

Fortune's Foot-Ball
Or, the adventures of Mercutio: founded on matters of fact. A novel. Part 1

ISBN/EAN: 9783337051754

Printed in Europe, USA, Canada, Australia, Japan

Cover: Foto ©Andreas Hilbeck / pixelio.de

More available books at **www.hansebooks.com**

FORTUNE's FOOT-BALL;

OR, THE

ADVENTURES

OF

MERCUTIO.

FOUNDED ON MATTERS OF FACT.

A NOVEL, IN TWO VOLUMES.

By JAMES BUTLER.

VOL. I.

HARRISBURGH, PENNSYLVANIA:
PRINTED BY JOHN WYETH.

1797.

PREFACE.

IN penning the following memoirs, I had no other object in view than my own amusement. This consideration may, perhaps, be accepted as an excuse for the familiarity of my ſtyle; which, as well as many other imperfections, will, no doubt, be perceived and condemned by the critic. The candid and indulgent reader, who reflects, that the piece was not till lately intended for the public eye—nor then, without the moſt urgent ſolicitations of a number of friends, will generouſly pardon any defect he may diſcover in the peruſal. Having been intimately acquainted with the hero of the piece, in my juvenile days, I can with confidence vouch for the authenticity of the narrative. 'Tis true, I have introduced ſome perſons and incidents which appear to be unconnected with the foundation of the ſtory; yet, it will be found, that were any of theſe withdrawn, the chain of events would be broken, and the congruity of the piece deſtroyed.—Upon the whole, if the ſtyle is not florid, it will not wound the ear of modeſty; if the ſubjects are not ſublime, they have a manifeſt tendency to propagate ſentiments of virtue—to ſtimulate youth to an humble reſignation to the diſpenſations of providence—and to diſcountenance vice.

At all events, I have ventured to lay it before the public, in hopes that, as a forlorn infant, it may find a foſter father, who will not ſuffer it to ſink in oblivion.

FORTUNE's FOOTBALL.

BEFORE I enter into a detail of the adventures of our hero, I presume it will not be unacceptable to my readers, if not expedient, to give a cursory sketch of his birth and education, in order to illustrate the subject of the following sheets. This I shall do in as concise a manner as possible—well knowing that prolixity creates disgust.

He was the first and only son of a gentleman in London, who enjoy'd an affluent and independent fortune—was noble, generous, humane and hospitable : His income not only supported his family in splendour, but also dispensed its glad'ning streams to the dreary abodes of pain and indigence. This gentleman, at a a suitable age, with the approbation of his friends, paid his addresses to a young lady of a distinguished family, and great fortune—possessed of every accomplishment to render a man of honour happy : To whom he was shortly married. Before the anniversary of their nuptials arrived, their happiness was augmented by the birth of a son, who, from that period; was the delight of every eye that saw him, and in whom all the rising hopes of his fond parents concentrated.

This son, is the person whose surprizing and variegated adventures I intend to disclose—candidly tracing him through the various mazes and doublings of his peregrination :——He was called Mercutio.

There is a period between infancy and manhood, in which, let our station in life be what it may, nothing but trifles occur : I should hold myself inexcusable in detaining the attention of my readers from the more interesting incident of my narrative, with an insipid relation of those ; and therefore, shall date the adventures of our hero from the commencement of his sixteenth year. At that period, he became enamoured with a young lady, by an accident, which laid the foundation of his future fortunes and misfortunes, and of course, this history.

He had just completed his studies, at Oxford, when he attained his sixteenth year : He therefore took leave of his teachers and fellow students, and repaired to London. It would be needless to describe the joyful emotions of his parents, on his arrival—Let it suffice to say, that while the fond mother clasp'd him with ardour to her bosom, his father's heart expanded with parental pride, to see his son—his only son, in full possession of every necessary accomplishment—nature as well as art having largely contributed to render him complete.

His mother, listen'd with supreme delight to the periods, which, with uncommon ease and propriety

he pronounced, while he defcribed the progrefs he had
made in his ftudies, and remark'd on the beauties and
deformities of the feveral authors which had come under his particular obfervation—which he did with fo
much judgment and candour, that envy herfelf could
have made no exception——She revolved in her mind
the many years of uninterrupted happinefs which it was
probable he might enjoy—the many hours of heart-felt
fatisfaction fhe herfelf, as well as his happy father were
yet likely to experience, not only in his company and
converfation, but alfo in the pleafing contemplation of
his tranfmitting his name and virtues to millions yet
unborn : But alas ! the happinefs of mankind is fleeting and tranfitory—like fair weather in an April day,
it is but of fhort duration ; and though fo widely different, from difappointment, pain and flavery, in its
nature and confequences, is, neverthelefs, fo immediately fucceeded by them, as to appear, to human con-
ception, to be of the fame family.

This happy family lived within fifteen minutes' walk
of Hyde-Park, and it being that delightful feafon of the
year in which nature feems to take a pride in difplaying
her innumerable beauties—our hero frequently walk'd
in the Park for recreation—fometimes in company with
his happy parents, and at others alone. As he delighted
much in reading, he feldom took an excurfion alone
without a book, in the perufal of which he often fpent
an hour or two—reclining beneath the friendly fhade
of fome one of thofe venerable trees which adorn that

fine Park. One evening, while he was amufing himfelf
in this manner, he was roufed by a fhriek of diftrefs,
which was uttered by a young lady, who, walking too
near the ferpentine river, where the bank was very
fteep, accidentally fell in—and the ftream running rapidly, wafh'd her more than a hundred yards in a few
feconds. Mercutio, being at a confiderable diftance
from the bank of the river, exerted his utmoft fpeed,
and perceiving the young lady juft above the water—
he plunged in—caught her in his arms, and with much
difficulty, bore her to the fhore, almoft breathlefs. He
was met at the bank of the river by two ladies, in tears,
who prov'd to be the mother and fifter of her he had
refcued from a watery grave. They gave him what
affiftance they could, in conveying her to a convenient
fituation, then requefted him to ftep to the end of Pic-
cadilly for an eminent phyfician, who lived there. He
ran immediately, leaving the young lady to the care of
her mother and fifter, and in a few words communicated his bufinefs to the furgeon : who inftantly accompanied him to the fpot. The young lady, notwithftanding the endeavours of her mother and fifter, was to
all appearance dead. The tender parent was hardly
kept from fainting, while the furviving daughter wept
immoderately—fo that the whole exhibited a fcene of
real diftrefs. While the furgeon exerted his abilities to
recover the almoft drowned lady, it required all the
philofophy as well as rhetoric of Mercutio, to keep the
other two in any tolerable degree of fpirits ;—however
it pleafed God to crown the endeavours of the furgeon

with unexpected fuccefs :—Cheerfulnefs diffufed itfelf inftantly over every countenance, when her refufcitation was announced—they furrounded her with an eagernefs which plainly indicated their late apprehenfions, and prefent fatisfaction. Our hero was not the laft in congratulating her on her recovery ; but the joy of her mother and fifter, is eafier imagined than defcribed. She, with a heavy figh, opened her eyes, which, even in that impair'd ftate, were equal in luftre to the diamond of the moft exquifite polifh, and looking around her, eagerly faid, where is my mama ?—Where is Charlotte ?——Here we are, replied the mother and fifter together. Be compofed, my dear, faid the old lady—Heaven has interpofed in our favour, and all will be well. Madam, interrupted the furgeon, my advice is to convey your daughter home as foon as poffible—let her be put in a warm bed, and do not difturb her to night—give me your addrefs, and I will vifit her early in the morning, and prefcribe fuch things as I fhall then judge falutary. The old lady returned her thanks for his care, and informed him that fhe lived on the fouth fide of Cavendifh-Square. The patient was then placed between her mother and fifter, in the doctor's chariot, which had brought him and Mercutio, who having promifed, at the inftance of the old lady, to accompany the furgeon the next day, took leave and departed.

Although the foregoing accident and adventure, does not appear to have been calculated for the foundation of an amour ; yet this was absolutely the cafe : For no sooner did Lucinda, (the young lady) expand her beauteous eyes, than love, like the electrical fire, diffus'd itself through each avenue of our hero's heart, which being tender and susceptible, retained this first impression so firmly, that it was never eradicated, until the lovely orbs, by which it was communicated, were quench'd in death.

Mercutio's mind had never been agitated before, in the same manner, as it was that evening, and the ensuing night. He slept little—broken slumbers, and confus'd ideas, tortur'd his imagination, till the return of the day. The image of Lucinda appear'd to his imagination in various forms : At one time, he beheld her pale and lifeless on the bank of the river—at another, faintly struggling with the impetuous stream—and sometimes as a bride, adorned for the nuptial ceremony, in all the bloom of youth, beauty and native innocence.

Having breakfasted, he hastened to the house of the surgeon, and with him, for the first time, rode to Cavendish-Square, where he was received with all that politeness peculiar to persons of exalted rank and refined education. Lucinda, after a comfortable night's rest, arose, invigorated and cheerful, and having been informed by her mama, of the particulars of what she had suffered the preceding evening, and of her miraculous preservation—she was just expressing her desire to see and thank her deliverer, when the servant announc'd the arrival of the phyfician and another gentleman. Lucinda's matchlefs charms blazed forth in their native fplendor—and, her natural vivacity having refumed its feat, her difcourfe confiderably encreafed the fatisfaction of the company. The old lady, acknowledged the prefervation of her daughter's life, in the moft grateful terms, and added, that fhe knew Lord S——r, her hufband, would never forget the obligation. Though our hero was fully recompenfed for the fervice he had rendered the daughter of Lord S——r, with a con-fcioufnefs of having been inftrumental in faving fuch a compofition of wit and beauty from the mercilefs jaws of death ; yet his fatisfaction was confiderably augmented, by the acknowledgments of Lucinda her-felf, which fhe expreffed in the following manner : Words, fir, are too weak, to defcribe my grateful fenfi-bility of the vaft obligation, under which, my mama informs me, you have laid me, by your humane exer-tions in faving me from impending danger ; but as the only return in my power at prefent, is a grateful re-membrance of the favour, I hope that may be accepted in part, and I promife to make up the deficiency, by ever efteeming you as the generous preferver of my life.

Madam, faid he, the reward you have promifed, and which I accept with joy, and fhall ever ftrive to deferve, is more than an equivalent to any fervice I could poffibly render ; but you muft not fuppofe yourfelf under any obligation to me ; for a gentleman who could have done lefs, on a fimilar occafion, muft have divefted himfelf of every particle of humanity, as well as violated its common laws.

The furgeon finding his fair patient in perfect health, and being fatisfied for his trouble, departed. Mercutio was more than once prevented from taking his leave, by the joint folicitations of the ladies, who ardently requefted the favour of his company till evening, to which he very willingly complied.

Dinner being over, the ladies played a duetto on the harpfichord, accompanied with their voices : The mafterly fkill with which they performed, and the enchanting harmony produced from the lips and fingers of thefe lovely girls, increafed the infant paffion of Mercutio to a degree of ardor not often exceeded. He liftened with rapture, and gazed with filent aftonifhment ! He had never feafted his eyes and ears fo fumptuoufly before. The evening approaching, he took leave, having previoufly, in compliance with reiterated requefts, promifed to renew his vifit fhortly, which he did not fail punctually to obferve, as will appear in the fequel.

As the accident which gave rife to our hero's acquaintance with this family, proved to be the fource of thofe furprizing adventures of which the enfuing part of this hiftory is compofed, I prefume it will not be accounted a digreffion, to prefent the reader with a very brief account of the eminent perfonages, who gave birth to the emprefs of his affections.

The father of Lucinda was the eldeſt ſon of the duke of N——, whoſe great abilities, as well in the field as cabinet, are too well known to need a repetition in this place: The ſon poſſeſſed not only the eſtate of his father, but alſo his virtues and bravery. At a ſuitable age, without having run through thoſe ſcenes of vice and diſſipation, which are too frequently and fatally the principal objects which our young noblemen purſue, he fixed his affections on an amiable young lady, daughter of Lord H——n. They lived, as might be expected, in all that harmony which never fails a virtuous union, founded on mutual eſteem. The firſt fruit of their connubial love was a daughter, which was the ſame who had captivated the affections of Mercutio. She had received an education ſuitable to her birth and fortune, which ſhe improved by every means poſſible. The ſecond child was a ſon, and called Charles, an amiable youth, then in Naples: He had been taken dangerouſly ill in that city, and his companion and tutor having written to his father, to inform him of the ſituation of his ſon, he had embarked, accompanied by a very able phyſician, for Italy.——But to return :——

Mercutio's attention was totally diverted from its uſual channel: 'twas entirely abſorbed in the contemplation of the charming qualifications of Lucinda, and in revolving the happy conſequences that would infallibly attend an honorable union with her—and began ſeriouſly to reſolve on matrimony, if the conſent of all

B

parties could be obtained : Of this, however, he had many doubts and fears ; having frequently heard his father reprobate the custom of marrying at too early a period, and being so young, he imagined would be an insurmountable obstacle in procuring his consent, which he conceived as absolutely necessary to his future happiness.

Lucinda's gratitude was, at the first interview, by an easy transition, converted to genuine friendship : It is no wonder, then, if the exact and manly features, symmetry of shape, engaging deportment, and natural vivacity of Mercutio, assisted by so powerful an ally as the most uncontaminated esteem, should have made an indelible impression on such a heart as her's—susceptible of the slightest. This was the case——but each was ignorant of the attachment of the other, and bore hard on the feelings of both ; for it would have afforded great consolation to them, to have known the real situation of each other's heart.

Mercutio resolved to love—he relinquished all his former diversions : The park, the ball, the opera and play, had no charms for him ! he devoted himself to solitude while at home—and seldom went abroad but to Lord S——'s.

It was at one of those visits he had the honour of his first interview with the father and brother of his beloved Lucinda. They had arrived from Italy the day before, both in health and vigour. On entering the room, Lu-cinda with a charming grace, taking his hand, prefented him to her father, faying, This, papa, is the gentleman (with the affiftance of heaven) to whom I owe this my fecond exiftence. He arofe inftantly, and enclofing him in his arms, faid, Sir, you have bound, by your generofity, me, and every branch of my family, by the moft lafting ties, thofe of friendfhip—let this day be the epocha of our invariable attachment. My dear Charles, faid he to his fon, from this day forward, confider this our worthy friend as a brother—a beloved and truly meritorious brother. So faying, he joined the hands of the two young men, who faluted each other with ardor. Mercutio congratulated his newly adopted brother, on his recovery and return to England ; and he, in return, affured him of his unfhaken gratitude and affection. They then entered into unreftrained converfation, in the courfe of which Mercutio's anxiety forfook him—he difcourfed with his ufual vivacity and good fenfe, and by his judicious reafoning and remarks, prov'd himfelf the finifhed gentleman. Charles was enraptured with his difcourfe, and earneftly wifhed to cultivate an acquaintance with one, whofe fentiments appeared congenial with his own, and who had already engroffed a large portion of his efteem.

In the afternoon, they took an excurfion in Hyde-Park, and coming to the fpot where Lucinda had flip-ped into the river, the gratitude of the whole family was again called into action : They reiterated their former

.acknowledgments, fo that Mercutio, overwhelmed with
a fenfe of their generofity, entreated them to defift, adding, that the favours he had received that day, were
fufficient to preponderate all he had done, or ever fhould
be able to do, though his whole future life fhould be
devoted to their fervice.   This turned the difcourfe in
another channel—for, as the whole family entertained
fentiments of the higheft efteem for him, they forebore
fpeaking on a fubject which they found gave him pain,
though they conceived themfelves fo highly obliged,
that they held themfelves infolvent.

Before they parted, Charles begged the favour of
Mercutio's company to Hampton court, on that day
week, adding, he had been fo long abroad that he had
almoft forgot the beautiful retreats of his own country.
Mercutio promifed to wait on him at the time appointed, and taking leave of the whole family, departed.—
His father, having fome affairs to tranfact at Briftol, fet
out the next morning for that place, while his fon
formed the refolution to difclofe his love for Lucinda
to his mother, before his father's return : Rightly judging, that if fhe approved, it would not be a very arduous tafk to procure his approbation alfo.   In confequence of this refolution, one evening, being engaged
in ferious converfation with her, he introduced the
important fecret that engroffed all his thoughts—and
caufed him fo much anxiety, and which he had never
communicated to any one before.   It happened that
his mother was not altogether unacquainted with the

family to which she found her son so firmly attached, and had he been of riper years, would not have withheld her approbation a moment ; but knowing her husband's tenacity in that point, she forebore giving a positive answer, for the present ; promising, however, to do every thing in her power, to interest his father in his behalf.

This, though insufficient immediately to obliterate every doubt, was a cordial to the mind of Mercutio : He, from that evening became cheerful, and before the day arriv'd on which he had consented to ride to Hampton, he enjoyed the most perfect tranquillity of mind, and resolved to acquaint his friend Charles, with the passion he had conceived for his eldest sister, but previously to enjoin him to secrecy, if he should disapprove of it. Having settled these things in his mind, he met his friend Charles at the appointed time and place. It was a fine day, and Charles entertained him with the many rarities and diversions of Italy, which afforded Mercutio much satisfaction. They arrived at Hampton about noon, and having refreshed, ordered dinner to be ready at three, and then went to regale themselves with the beauties of the elegant gardens which pertain to the palace.

After ranging those spacious and delightful avenues for some time, the keeper appear'd, to conduct them into the Labyrinth, which is a master-piece of ingenuity : It is so very intricate, that it is next to an impossibility for a person, unacquainted with its various turnings and windings, being once fairly entered, to extricate himself without the affiftance of a guide. Thofe youths having entered, the keeper retired, but remained within call, well knowing they would have need of his affiftance. Having attained the centre, they fat down under a fine fhady tree to reft, and to difcourfe till it fhould be time to go to dinner. After fome preparatory converfation, Mercutio, in a few words, and in a very diffident ftyle, informed Charles of his violent paffion for Lucinda, and requefted him to give his opinion and advice on the fubject, as it was a very important one to him. My dear friend, faid Charles, it gives me infinite pleafure, that the perfon whom I fo much efteem, has honoured me with his confidence in a matter fo weighty and interefting, and muft freely confefs, that it is no more than I fufpected. I have, fince my return from Italy, obferved a degree of fingularity in my fifter's behaviour, which gave birth to that fufpicion : She devotes much of her time to folitude—appears remarkably penfive—except when you honour us with your company, at which time fhe refumes her native fprightlinefs ; but no fooner are you gone, than fhe retires to her chamber, and feldom appears cheerful till a fimilar occafion prefents itfelf. My fifter Charlotte has alfo made the fame remark, which fhe communicated to me, and imputes it to the real caufe, namely, Love : And to give you my fentiments freely on the fubject, I really believe Lucinda to be under the fame perplexities you labour under yourfelf. But tell me, my dear Mercutio, have you ever difclofed your

paſſion to my ſiſter ? No, my dear friend, your virtuous
—your accompliſhed ſiſter is yet unacquainted with the
flame which preys each moment on my heart, and this
it is that has rendered me unhappy :—Unhappy ! exclaimed Charles, I ſhould hold myſelf guilty of ingratitude, and conſequently unworthy your friendſhip, if I
could harbour the moſt diſtant idea of your being unhappy without ſympathizing with you, and contributing all in my power to reſtore your peace of mind :
—My ſiſter, or I am much miſtaken, loves you ardently, My advice is, that you reveal your ſentiments to her
without delay—for I am fully ſenſible that there is not
one of the family, but would be proud of the alliance :
—Baniſh every apprehenſion—explain yourſelf without
reſerve, and my life for it, you'll ſucceed. For my part,
you may depend on all the aſſiſtance in my power—
but my opinion is, you have a friend in the citadel,
that will do more execution than all the external aux-
iliaries you can command.

Mercutio was ſo overwhelmed with a ſenſe of his
friend's uncommon generoſity, that he was for ſome
time at a loſs for words to deſcribe his own feelings on
the occaſion.——My ineſtimable friend, ſaid he, where
have you imbibed this greatneſs of ſoul? Your good-
neſs is ſo unlimited, that there is not a bare poſſibility
of a retaliation—but rely on my unchangeable attachment—my willingneſs to embrace every opportunity of
rendering you all the ſervice in my power——Come,
come, ſaid Charles, haſtily interrupting him, no more

of this—let's away to dinner. Mercutio, looking at his watch, found it was four. They started up inflantly, and walked almoſt an hour at a good round rate, when to their amazement, they found themſelves juſt where they had been ſitting ſo long—they attempted it again, but without ſuccefs—they were conſtrained to call the keeper, who liberated them in a few minutes.

They haſtened to the inn, where they found dinner waiting—their walk having created good appetites, they ate heartily ; and after taking a cheering glaſs, remounted, and ſet out for London. Night overtook them about three miles from town, and as they were riding ſlowly along, buſy in diſcourfe, they were met by a youth, genteely dreſſed, and well mounted, who preſenting a piſtol to Mercutio's breaſt, demanded his money.

Their ſervants being armed, rode up and took him, which was eaſily accompliſhed, as he made no reſiſt-ance ; but exclaimed aloud—Now, my miſeries will foon have an end ! I ſhall die contented, and my dear Amelia will ſee that I prefer even an ignominious death, to a wretched life, without her !—Theſe words ſurprized our young friends—they both wiſhed to know the cauſe of this young highwayman's inconſiſtent behaviour. The ſervants had bound him, and were riding one on each ſide, when Mercutio and Charles halted——The words and actions of this young man, ſaid Mercutio, ſurprize me exceedingly—I feel deſirous to know what has prompted him to take to the highway—in my opinion, he is but a novice in the trade; for instead of attempting an escape, he appeared willing to be taken, and by the words he expressed while the servants were binding him, I suspect this action the effect of a desperate resolution, formed in consequence of some disappointment in a love affair—I think it would be worth our while to examine him on the subject. You have utter'd my sentiments exactly, replied Charles—I think there must be something very singular in his case; for as you observed, he does not appear to have had much experience. They soon overtook their company, and ordering their servants to ride forward, took charge of the prisoner themselves.

My friend, said Mercutio, what could induce you, among such a variety of occupations which exist in this kingdom, to make choice of one, which must inevitably terminate in ignominy and punishment?

That question, said the prisoner, stabs me to the soul. He paused—and would have said no more, had not Mercutio desired him to inform them by what means he had been reduced to that way: You need not, said he, be under apprehension of any circumstance, which you may probably discover in your narrative, being brought against you before a magistrate—for you may depend upon our honour, that whatever you disclose to us, shall be buried in eternal oblivion—and for this reason we sent our servants forward: Therefore, by giving us a brief and candid relation of the misfortunes

or temptations, which, perhaps, contrary to your
natural inclination, precipitated you into this dangerous course, may have a palliative tendency, and your
affairs, however unpromising at present, may shortly
terminate in your favour.

If you mean, returned the prisoner, that it will have
a tendency to divert your intentions of surrendering me
into the hands of justice, I should willingly refuse, be-
cause a person who has no business in this world, should
stay no longer in it than to procure a convenient passage
to another, which however bad, cannot be worse than
this ; and as I am one of this description, am willing
to meet death in any form and at any time.   But, gentlemen, you appear to be generous, and therefore,
whatever pangs the relation of my late misfortunes
may add to my tortured soul, I shall endeavour to gratify your request.

My father is a merchant of no small account, in the
city which now lies before us.   My mother died when
I was about eleven years of age, and I being the only
child, was placed at Rule's academy, at Islington,
where I remained two years ; when a brother of my
mother's, having repeatedly urged my father to send
me to one of the universities, without success, took me
from thence and placed me at Oxford, where, after
making ample provision for my education, &c. took
an affectionate leave, previously exhorting me to be
diligent, and obedient to my tutors—If you are at-

tentive to your studies, said he, you shall find you have
at least one friend. My kind uncle was as good as his
word—for he took the most scrupulous pains to have
me well accommodated for the space of five years,
which was the time I remained at the univerfity. When
I had finished my studies, I returned to London, and
after returning my affectionate thanks to my worthy
uncle, for his care of my education, as well as many
other favours, I waited on my father, who received me
very kindly. Well, George, said he, I understand you
intend to practice law ; but I wish you would wave
that refolution for the present, as I have great need of
your affiftance—befides, it may be of fervice to you
hereafter, to have a thorough knowledge of the mercan-
tile branch. He paufed——I told him to command
me in any thing he pleafed, and I would convince him,
that in my long abfence I had not forgot to pay the
moft refpectful obedience to his orders. This anfwer
pleafed him exceedingly—and from that day to this,
I have tranfacted his bufinefs with the greateft care and
punctuality. But how shall I relate the reft ?—Some
time ago, I conceived a tendernefs for an amiable young
creature, the only daughter of a very wealthy jeweller,
in Cheapfide : This tendernefs encreafed rapidly, and
was foon fucceeded by the moft ardent paffion. I declared my fuferings to the dear object of my wishes—
who condefcended to approve, and accepted my vows.
Our love became reciprocal. But—fince that fatal
moment, anxiety has been my infeparable companion.
Our fathers happened to have fentiments congenial—

yet it was impoffible ever to obtain their mutual confent
to our union—as they had both formed a determination
never to agree to the marriage of their children with
any perfon, but fuch as had a great fortnne, and im-
bib'd principles fimilar to their own—and were refolved never to part with a fhilling, until death fhould
deprive them of the power of accumulating wealth.

Under fuch circumftances, conceive, if you can,
the torment we endured. Buoyed up with flattering
hopes, however, and having frequent opportunities of
enjoying each other's company, our fituation was yet
tolerable; but alas! this was but of fhort duration.
My father, yefterday evening, came into the compting-
houfe, and appeared remarkably pleafant :—After fome
preliminary difcourfe—George, faid he, I am furprized
that a young fellow of your lively turn don't endeavor
to pufh yourfelf into the world ;—I mean, continued
he, by marriage. There is nothing gives a young man
fo great an opportunity of making a fortune as an ad-
vantageous match. Why, before I was of your age,
there was not a great fortune, maid or widow, in town,
or within twenty miles round it, but I paid my addreffes
to—and you fee what an eftate I have raifed from your
mother's dowry. You underftand the law, and if you
was married to a woman of fortune, you might, with
the help of her gold, foon climb the ladder of prefer-
ment—might foon be lord chief juftice, my boy.

I was aftonifhed at his difcourfe, as I had frequently, fince I left college, heard him reprobate a married life as being attended with great expence, care and anxiety, and declaring, that if he was a young man, he never would be duped into it again. However, I told him I had often thought of matrimony, and fhould have no objection to it, with an agreeable young woman. As to her being agreeable, faid he, I fuppofe you mean handfome, or young—thefe are but fecondary confiderations: The woman whom I would recommend fhould be rich—if handfome it would be no objection ; but for age, it fignifies not a button. Now I have taken the pains to felect a woman for you, to whom in my opinion, you cannot have the leaft objection—fhe's none of your foolifh, extravagant jillflirts, who would ruin you in paint, patches and lace :—No, no, my boy, fhe's a fober, ftaid body, induftrious and frugal—true, fhe's about forty or forty-five ; but then fhe has twenty-five thoufand pounds in glittering gold, my boy: and the greateft advantage of all is, fhe'll not have many children. Now, George, what do you think of my propofal ?—What do you think you are indebted to me for anticipating your very hopes—and providing fuch a wife for you ?

I was fo confounded with this laft fpeech, that for fome time I was unable to anfwer him ; but recovering myfelf a little from the vexation I felt, I obferved, that I was deeply fenfible of his goodnefs, in procuring fuch a perfon as he had defcribed ; but thought it proba-

C

ble the lady's affections might be pre-engaged, as I had never been honoured with an interview——Not at all, not at all, interrupted my father, haſtily : People of ſenſe never ſuffer their affections to be engaged contrary to their intereſt :—She knows I have no child but you, and conſequently, that you will be very rich at my deceaſe : You need not be under any apprehenſion on that ſcore—I'll introduce you to-morrow, and my word for it, you'll meet with no repulſe. I replied, my dear father; I am ſorry it is out of my power to accept the honour you intended me—as I am engaged to a perſon of ſuch beauty and good ſenſe, that you yourſelf muſt applaud my choice, and——A damn'd proſtitute, interrupted he, in great rage—ſome offspring of extravagance and folly, I dare ſay ; but I dont care who or what ſhe is—if you don't acquieſce with my proproſal, prepare to turn out, for here you'll ſtay no longer, nor ever finger one penny of my eſtate, I promiſe you :—I would ſooner bequeath it to my grave-digger. Let me have a final anſwer to-morrow morning ;—but, d'ye hear, I will be obey'd, one way or other.

With theſe words he left me to the moſt mortifying reflections. I remained petrified with aſtoniſhment for ſome time ; but at length reſolved to pay my dear Amelia a viſit to inform her of my deplorable ſituation. and urge her to accompany me to my uncle's, where I knew we ſhould be received with affection, and there tie the indiſſoluble knot, which would forever fruſtate the caprice of an unfeeling parent. With thefe perplexing ideas, I reached her father's, who, to my inexpreffible anguifh, would not permit me to fee her. You muft difcontinue your vifits here, faid he—my daughter is to be married in a few days to Mr. Ephraims of the old Jewry, a wealthy broker. I was juft going to folicit a moment's interview—but he cut me fhort— George, it's needlefs for you to put yourfelf to any further trouble about her, as it will be impoffible for you to fee her until fhe is married to Mr. Ephraims, who is now with her in the dining-room : Come, will you take a walk to the coffee-houfe ? I made him no anfwer, but taking my hat and cane, left the room, pronouncing the words DAMNED AVARICE ! I returned home in dreadful perturbation of mind, threw myfelf on the bed in all the pangs of defpair. I flept none— but waited the return of day, with an anxiety not to be defcribed.

I went this morning to the compting-houfe, as ufual, though undetermined what anfwer to give my father. He did not fuffer me to deliberate long ; for coming in fuddenly, he demanded my anfwer, with a countenance which indicated his difpleafure, and the ftorm impend- ing, which foon burft upon my devoted head :—Don't hefitate a moment, young man, faid he, I'm not to be trifled with. In the tumult which then pervaded my foul, I told him, I had given all the anfwer I had to give :—Then, you infamous fcoundrel, faid he, begone out of my houfe inftantly—you unworthy rafcal ! if ever I catch you within my doors again, I'll shoot you. I rose inftantly, and he thruft me out the door, in a degree of rage bordering on madnefs.

In the height of my defpair, I took the fatal refolution which you have juft witneffed. I hired this horfe at a livery ftable where I was known, in order to be difco- vered, and fet out in the dufk of evening——The reft you know; but when I attacked you, my wifh was, that you would have lodged a friendly bullet in my head, and rid the world of the unhappieft of mortals. Here he ftopped, when Mercutio, with fome earneftnefs, demanded his name :—My name, replied he, is George Wright. Gracious heavens! exclaimed Mercutio, is it poffible that you are my friend and fellow-ftudent, with whom I have fpent fo many delightful hours at Ox- ford? Have you forgot Mercutio?—Mercutio! re- turned he, greatly agitated, is this you? No, it is im- poffible for me to forget him—but long abfence, and the extreme confufion of mind, had almoft obliterated from my memory every trace of thofe well known features——Oh Mercutio! did you ever expect to fee what you have this evening?—Tears forbid further utterance. He was immediately unbound, while Mer- cutio and Charles endeavoured both by moral and phi- lofophical arguments to diffuade him from his defperate purpofe—in which they happily fucceeded. Mercutio offered him his purfe, which he refufed—faying, I have money enough : If that would purchafe happinefs, I need not be long without it. Being now pretty late,

when they reached Hyde-Park wall, and having exact-
ed a promise from George, that he would not attempt
to shorten his days, either directly or indirectly, they
parted, each taking a different route.

The next day, Mercutio paid a visit to Lucinda,
and Charles having introduced him, retired. She received his visit with manifest marks of satisfaction on
her countenance, which inspired her lover to avow his
passion with confidence, which he did in the most unequivocal, yet respectful terms, and received an answer,
which totally eradicated every sentiment of anxiety
from his breast,—the most perfect tranquillity pervaded
his soul. His father having returned from Bristol,
he communicated his case to him in a letter, couched in
the most submissive and respectful terms—relating, without reserve, every circumstance which had occurred
in the first of his seeing the beautiful object of his love,
until that day, and finally requesting permission to continue his addresses to the young lady. This letter he
committed to the care of his mother, who was to negociate the matter for him. Having dispatched this
part of the business, it was necessary to communicate
his wishes to the parents of Lucinda. This he resolved
to do in person : Accordingly, he summoned up all
his fortitude, and waited on them for that purpose. He
was received with the same degree of kindness which
he had experienced ever since his acquaintance in that
family. When the common topics of the day were dif-
cussed, the ladies withdrew, leaving him, Charles and the

C 2

father together. After a fhort preface, Mercutio informed lord S——— the motive of his vifit, and earneftly
folicited his permiffion to addrefs his eldeft daughter on
the fubject of marriage. His reply was fuch as might
have been expected :—I fhould hold myfelf ungrateful
in the higheft degree, faid he, and confequently highly
culpable, if not unpardonable, were I to deny your
requeft ; but fo far from that, I grant it with pleafure,
as to a perfon, of all others, the moft deferving : and, I
miftake, or Lucinda herfelf is of the fame opinion.
Mercutio made a fuitable acknowledgment of the honour done him, adding, that the pleafure he experienced on the prefent occafion, could only be exceeded by
that which he muft derive from the abfolute confummation of the defired union.

Not to trouble the reader with a repetition of all the
tender epithets, and languifhing fpeeches, infeparable
from negociations of this kind—let it fuffice to fay,
that matters were in a fhort time fo forward, that the marriage articles were drawn—a day appointed for the
celebration of the nuptials, and the two families united
in the ftricteft amity. So far, then, had Mercutio been
fuccefsful ; nay, fo flattering was the profpect, that he
would not have relinquifhed his claim, to have been
made emperor of the world. But, alas ! the period
was approaching, with hafty ftrides, in which the moft
gloomy fadnefs was to ufurp dominion over the empire
of his foul—when all thofe gilded fcenes which then
prefented themfelves to the eye of his imagination, were

to "diffolve, and like the bafelefs fabric of a vifion, leave not a wreck behind."

A few days previous to that appointed for the wedding, Lucinda was attacked with an extreme pain in her left breaft and fide. A phyfician being called, fhe was let blôod, and was, apparently, in a fair way of recovery ; but the enfuing night, fhe was feized with an intermittent fever ; and, in nine days, in fpite of the moſt ſkilful and ſtrenuous endeavours of feveral of the faculty, eminent in their profeffion, the beauteous Lucinda refigned her immortal parts into the hands of Him who gave it, reclining in the arms of her difconfolate lover, who had fcarcely eat, drank or flept, or even left the houfe, during her illnefs.

This was a fevere ſtroke to the afflicted Mercutio! Yet well calculated to teach him refignation to the will of the Almighty. She was interred in the family vault in St. James's church, on the very day her hand was to have been joined to Mercutio's, who followed her remains, array'd in folemn black, which but faintly expreffed the gloomy fituation of his mind.

Having affifted at thofe rites, which forever feparated him from that treafure, which but a few days before, not all the riches of the eaft would have purchafed, he betook himfelf to the moſt profound folitude—kept no company—never went abroad, except to fpend a lonefome hour in St. James church. One morning early, when he repaired to that awful receptacle, and having walked backward and forward for some time, with his arms folded together, suppofing himfelf alone, broke out into the following paffionate exclamations : Oh ! my tortured bofom !—Where fhall my foul find peace ? Alas, there is none for me on this fide eternity—no, no, the marble jaws of death hath feparated, finally feparated me from all the world contained to render me happy ! I fhall never more behold thofe ravifhing features which once tranfported my devoted foul!—where blooming innocence and inimitable beauty contended for pre-eminence—fhall never liften to thofe joy-infpiring accents, which has fo frequently fill'd my foul with pleafure unfpeakable ! But though the cruel tyrant has feparated our bodies, our fouls can never be divided— that tie is too ftrong—it cannot—fhall not be broken. Here, Charles, who had arrived at the mournful fpot before Mercutio, and had heard the foregoing, difcovered himfelf. Though the time, place and other circumftances, had a palpable tendency to render folitude more folitary ; yet it was a matter of confolation to thofe young friends to meet, even on fo mournful an occafion : For though it was impoffible for one to remove the melancholy from the other, yet by intermingling their griefs, they were enabled to fupport the enormous load more patiently, than they could have done feparately. After difcourfing fome time on the fhortnefs and pofitive certainty of the extinction, fooner or later, of human life, as well as the innumerable avenues leading to the gloomy manfions of death, that are conftantly

crouded with perfons of all ranks, ages, fex, and de-
nominations, travelling to the never-ending regions of
eternity—they found themfelves inperceptibly betrayed
into a train of cheerful ideas, (the natural confequence
of moral and religious difcourfes) and their melancholy
retreated infenfibly. In this frame of mind, Mercutio
requefted Charles to fpend the day with him. Taking
leave of that awful recefs, they dropt a tributary tear
and departed. They fpent the day in a manner corre-
fponding with that in which they had began it, taking
to their affiftance HERVEY and SHERLOCK, whofe
inimitable works made no fmall addition to that cheerful refignation with which their morning difcourfe had
infpired them.

Thus did thofe young men, adopt the moft proper
meafure imaginable, to fruftrate the fecret wiles of the
great adverfary of mankind, who is ever ready, on fuch
occafions, to fuggeft doubts of the providence of God,
whereby the afflicted, or rather tempted perfons, are
fometimes prompted to precipitate themfelves into ir-
retrievable ruin, by rufhing, uncall'd-for, into the awful and immediate prefence of God, " with all their
imperfections on their heads."

Mercutio, finding no relifh for the reigning pleafures
of the town, and being conftantly importuned to accompany the youthful and gay in diverfions, which to
him were difgufting, refolved to travel, if it fhould
meet the approbation of his parents. He accordingly

proposed it to them—they freely assented, in hopes
that a diversity of climate, and the innumerable objects,
both natural and artificial, to be met with in making
the tour of Europe, might have a happy effect in re-
viving those animated marks of a cheerful heart and
vigorous body, which had ever been the leading features
in his countenance, until impaired by grief and disappointment.

Preparations were made for his intended voyage:
He visited the parents of the much lamented Lucinda.
But, it would require some of the finest strokes and
strongest colouring that ever proceeded from the pen of
the immortal Raphael, to paint the emotions of the
whole family, when the moment of separation arrived.
Not an eye present but shed the tear of real affection!
Not a heart but palpitated, in perfect unison, with the
soul-dividing pangs of separation.   Lord S—— and
his amiable consort, clasp'd their departing friend to
their noble breasts, in all the extacy of parental love.
Adieu! my dear son they exclaimed together. Adieu!
my beloved friend and brother, repeated Charles and
Charlotte——It was too much for human nature to
bear——The organs of speech were mutually arrested
—tears supplied the place of words. He silently and
speedily withdrew, while his agitated limbs were yet
capable of supporting him out.

After taking an affectionate leave of his parents, he
set out post for Dover, and embarked on board a packet

at that place, attended by two trusty domestics, who had been many years in the family, and arrived at Calais the same evening. It is more than probable, that if Mercutio, or his friends, had barely conceived the danger, difficulties, hardships and slavery, he had to encounter, before they were to meet again, they would have guarded against so fatal an event with all their powers ; but it is more wisely order'd : man is not permitted to penetrate the unfathomable depths of futurity: he is allow'd a faint glimpse of the present : and, while he retains his faculties, he may, by retro-spection, take an imperfect, ideal view, of such of the past as has been strongly marked, and consequently made a more lasting impression than generally attend the common occurrences of life ; but the incidents and objects of futurity are concealed behind an impenetra-ble cloud, until the unceasing, undeviating order of nature, shall unfold them, individually, in the order in which they may then lie.

He made no stay in Calais, but proceeded to Paris. As he had not much relish for conversation, he intended, while he resided in Paris, to act the part of a spectator only : Of course, he took lodgings at a private house, in a pleasant situation, where he could enjoy the cool air, undisturb'd by the rattling of chariots, and the vain pomp of Parisian grandeur. He attended all pub-lic places of recreation, but carefully avoided culti-vating an intimacy with any person. He wrote to his father and other friends, by every post : This, and the perufal of the feveral epiftles from them, (not one of whom neglected to anfwer punctually every one of his) employed moft of his leifure time, and afforded him much of that kind of pleafure, in which he then moft delighted.

Being prefent at an auction of pictures, one day, where feveral perfons of diftinction were affembled, his eyes involuntarily caught a face which feem'd familiar to him : He fixed his attention on the object, and after confidering him for fome minutes, found it to be his old acquaintance and fellow-ftudent, George Wright. Mercutio was a good deal furprized at feeing him in that place, and fo richly dreffed (it being an elegant fuit, fafhioned in the Parifian tafte, and richly embroidered) in fo fhort a time after the fingular affair before recited. He found means to difcover himfelf to his friend, who, when he recognized him, gave a fignal to follow, and immediately left the room. When they had got into the ftreet, Georg , in a very affectionate manner, took Mercutio by the hand, faying, I have joyful news to communicate to you, my dear friend ; but we will ftep into a hotel, where we can difcourfe in private, and with freedom. There being one within a few fteps, they entered, when George called for a private room and a bottle of Burgundy. I make no doubt, faid George, but you are aftonifhed at the alteration you perceive in me—but banifh your furprize : T   dear girl, of whom I told you the laft time I had the happinefs of feeing you in England, and whom I confidered as irrecoverably loft to me, is now in Paris, and mine by every law, human and divine, and death alone can feparate us. Why, you have been very fortunate indeed, replied Mercutio. Fortunate ! Yes, my friend, my good fortune has exceeded my moft fanguine expectations ; and, be affured, my heart vibrates with gratitude to heaven, and you, the happy inftrument of my falvation from eternal infamy and defpair ! Mercutio expreffing a wifh to be informed of the particulars of this apparently unaccountable revolution, George proceeded to gratify it. After I parted with you and your friend at Hyde-Park wall, I went to a friend in whom I could confide, and related my ftory in a few words, concealing only the refolution I had taken in confequence of my father's barbarity, and requefted his advice and affiftance. Why, faid he, it's a critical affair —I'm at a lofs how to advife——After a fhort paufe— George, faid he, I'll tell you what—I will go in the morning to your father, and, without taking any notice of having feen you, as I am fomething in his debt, fettle and pay him off : Then, as he will be obliged to examine the account himfelf, I fhall have a fair opportunity to enquire for you, if he does not ftart it himfelf. This will naturally (as you know our intimacy) bring out the whole tranfaction, in which I fhall be able to difcover how the old man ftands affected towards you. If I find him relenting, I will immediately prefs him to a reconciliation—if not, I fhall be filent on the fubject : This is all in my power to do, in the prefent ftate of affairs. In the morning he fet out—and it is hard to

D

determine whether hope or fear was moft predominant
in my foul during his abfence ; but one thing is certain,
that I never fuffered fo much uneafinefs in fo fhort a
time before. At length he returned—and, to my extreme
amazement, announced the inftantaneous death of my
father ! And though it might be fuppofed, after expe-
riencing fuch cruel treatment, I fhould receive the news
of his deceafe with a degree of fatisfaction, rather than
regret :—But I do affure you, this was not the cafe—
I ftood aftonifhed for fome time, and know not how
long I fhould have remained fo, had not my friend
rouzed me from my reverie, by telling me, my prefence
was abfolutely neceffary at home, as my father was a
widower, and having no child but me, the affairs of the
family would otherwife foon fall into a diftracted ftate.
Befides, what would the world fay, if you fhould fo far
neglect your duty, as not to provide for and fuperintend
your father's funeral ?—Although I was fully fenfible
of the juftice and propriety of thefe hints—yet I was fo
wrapt in the contemplation of the fudden ftroke which
had reduced my father to a ftate of inanimation, that I
had forgot every thing elfe. However, not to detain
you, I repaired home, where I no fooner perceived him
from whom I derived my exiftence, lying pale and
breathlefs, than, impelled by filial love and duty, I fell
on the venerable corpfe, and bathed it with tears—
lamenting, in the moft fincere and pathetic terms, his
premature death, which was occafioned by a fit of
apoplexy. To be brief—in one month after the funeral
obfequies were performed, in confequence of a letter

from my uncle in Venice, requesting me to go thither, I applied myself to the settling my affairs, which to me who had managed my father's business so long, was an easy matter.

Upon the whole, after settling and paying every legal demand, I found myself worth at least forty thousand pounds. Among a number of bonds, which I discovered in a little box in my father's scrutoire, one for five and twenty hundred pounds, on the father of my dear Amelia presented itself. I wrote to him without delay, informing him of my intended voyage to Venice, and requesting immediate payment. The next day, I received an answer to my billet, full of consolatory language, expressing much sorrow for the loss I had sustained in so good a father—requesting the favour of a visit, and added, that he could not reimburse the whole sum for a few weeks, owing to some heavy losses he had met with in the public funds, &c.

As I wished for nothing on earth so much as one more interview with his daughter, if yet unmarried, should it even be the last—a gleam of hope darted thro' my soul, and suggested the idea, that if she was yet single, I might one day be so happy as to call her mine.

I waited on the old man in a few days. He received me with much apparent kindness, and to my inexpressible joy, introduced me to his daughter, as beautiful, and as much at liberty as when I last parted with her—

though her father had employed the most rigorous
means to force her to wed the avaricious, superannuated
Israelite—yet it was all to no purpose—the lovely
girl remained inflexible ; she chose rather to endure
confinement, nay, even death itself, than submit to be
joined to a wretch of that description. In the course
of our conversation, I gave him to understand, that I
should have immediate occasion for the money, as I
intended to embark for Venice in a few days, having
settled all my affairs, and that a failure would be de-
trimental, and perhaps productive of disagreeable consequences. He told me, he would endeavour to furnish it within three weeks, and concluded with a request,
that I would not pass his door as a stranger, in the
mean time ; for as he ever had a great veneration for
my deceased father, he should think it an honour to
be ranked among the friends of his son.

It was easy to perceive the old fellow's drift. He
was well acquainted with my father's circumstances,
and also, that I was sole heir ; therefore, he conceived
if he could ingratiate himself with me, I would not only
marry his daughter without a portion, but also release
him from the payment of the bond, in which he was
not altogether mistaken ; for finding her attachment as
strong as ever, I · `s determined to renew my visit
shortly, and demand her of her father in marriage, and
if granted, I was resolved to have celebrated as soon as
possible, without regard to the motives or conditions of
his consent. In short, at the very next visit I declared

myself to him. He confented without hefitation, and
in ten days more, heaven conferred on me the greateft
bleffing—my every wifh. We were married, and the
fame day I refigned the bond into his own hands, without any confideration, which pleafed him exceedingly.
George, faid he, you have been a dutiful fon to your de-
ceafed father, and for that reafon I have given you my
only child, and though I have given her nothing on the
day of her marriage, all I have will fall to you both
when I die, and perhaps I fhall make as great an addition to my prefent ftock, as you could poffibly, if you
had it in your own hands.

I immediately made the neceffary preparations for
my intended voyage. Having never been in France, I
refolved, in order to fhow my dear Amelia the manners
of the Parifians, as well as gratify my own curiofity,
to take it in my tour: We have been here a month,
and expect to fail for Italy in a few days.—This is all I
have to communicate at prefent. Now, I wifh you to
accompany me to my lodgings, where, as long as
we remain in Paris, you fhall be a welcome gueft.
Mercutio confented, and on the way informed George
of his own fad difafter, and of the refolution he had
taken in confequence. George fympathized with him
in his misfortunes; but at the fame time, begged him to
be confoled: for, it argues a debility of mind, to faint
under the difpenfations of providence ;—true fortitude,
you have taught me, confifts in a virtuous and cheerful refignation: It is to your animating and well-timed

D 2

instructions, I owe all my present and future happiness; but for them, I might ere now, have suffered an ignominious death. I beg you will not take amiss what I so freely say, as it proceeds from a sincere desire to see · you happy; for you may rest assured, there is not a man upon earth, who shares with you an equal proportion of my esteem. No, replied Mercutio, so far from it, that I deem it as a particular mark of friendship. Mrs. Wright gave her new visitor a cordial reception. She was very handsome, and possessed a sufficient share of good sense, so that he was very happy in having met with such agreeable company, and hearing much of the beauty and pleasant situation of Venice, which is situated on seventy-two small islands, in the Adriatic gulph, resolved to accompany his friend thither.

Having dispatched a letter home to advertise his friends of his intention, he embarked on board an Italian ship, bound to Rome, whither they had a short and pleasant passage. After staying three days in that once fam'd capital, to refresh, they set out by land for Ancona, from whence they sailed in a small vessel for Venice. On their arrival, they found George's uncle in good health, who received Mercutio with the greatest politeness imaginable. He was at first, overjoyed to see his nephew; but his transport was much abated, when he was informed of the sudden death of his brother.

Mercutio, at the earneſt requeſt of the whole family, took up his abode with them during his ſtay at Venice. He viſited all the iſlands in the republic, and every place of public reſort in each, ſo that at length he reſumed his former vivacity, and began to entertain a reliſh for ſociety. The tranquillity of his mind appeared viſible on his countenance, and he frequently mingled with the young Venetians of quality, in the diverſions peculiar to that country,

The Doge having given an invitation to all the youth of diſtinction in the city (to partake of a ſplendid entertainment to be given in honour of the Doge of Naples, who had arrived, with a great retinue, on a viſit) with liberty to introduce all their foreign friends and acquaintances of the ſame deſcription. Mercutio was preſſed by a young Venetian of the firſt rank to accompany him. He complied, and had the honour of dancing with the Doge's daughter, beautiful as Venus, but not a Diana. He was ſtruck with the brilliancy of her charms, but was ignorant of her quality—yet ſuppoſed her the daughter of ſome great perſonage. The higheſt encomiums were beſtowed on him and his incomparable partner by the two Doges, who were preſent during the whole entertainment. 'Twas late when the company retired, and Mercutio having juſt turned the corner of the ſtreet where he lodged, was overtaken by a young female, who delivered him a billet, the ſubſtance of which was couched in the following terms:

STRANGER,

HAVING been fo happy as to be honored with your hand this evening, I have, for a peculiar reafon, a ftrong defire to have a fhort interview in private, as I have a matter of great importance to communicate to you. If this meets your approbation, you will attend vefpers to-morrow evening, at the chapel of St. Aloyfius, where the perfon who delivers this will attend, to conduct you to a proper place for that pur-pofe—if not, deftroy this, and quit Venice fpeedily—Perhaps you may find no reafon to repent a compliance.

Mercutio having got home, examined the billet, and perufed it attentively feveral times over, juftly conclud-ed it muft be the lady with whom he danced, that had honored him with this fingular epiftle. The next morn-ing he fhowed the billet to George, and requefted his advice, adding, he would fain meet the author, if he thought he might do it with fafety. Why, replied he, I don't imagine you have any caufe to apprehend dan-ger in meeting her; but a refufal, it appears to me, if you remain here, may be attended with difagreeable confequences. If I was in your place, I would meet her at all events. In confequence of this advice, he attended at the time and place appointed, where he had not been long, before he obferved a female, whom he thought the fame that delivered him the paper. She feemed very bufy in examining the features of the whole congregation; at length, fixing her eyes on him for fome time, and having fatisfied herfelf as to the identity of his perfon, her folicitude vanifhed, and fhe contented herfelf with a flight glance now and then. It was growing dufk when vefpers ended, yet he ftill obferved the female loitering about till the congregation was difperfed—fhe then beckoned him to follow her. He complied—and without fpeaking a word, followed her through many turnings and windings, and juft as the day clofed, they arrived at a fmall wicket, which opened into a fpacious garden. His conductrefs having admitted him, locked the gate, and conducted him to an elegant fummer-houfe, where, in a whifper fhe told him he muft wait a few moments, while fhe went to inform her miftrefs of his arrival—and departed inftantly.

While he was ruminating on the fingularity of his prefent fituation, his attention was fuddenly diverted by the ruftling of filk, advancing towards the place where he fat. He rofe, and advanced to falute her— fhe unveiled at his approach, and returned his falute with ardor. She prevented him from fpeaking by faying :—Your condefcention, fir, has exceeded my expectations, which induces me to draw the moft flattering prefage of our future correfpondence. My prefent conduct may, perhaps, appear to have an air of levity ; but I hope I fhall be able to juftify it to you, at leaft ; for though cuftom has rendered it criminal for a female to make advances towards the other fex ; yet nature and reafon mutually confpire, to render a difpenfation with this tyrannical cuftom abfolutely neceffary, in fome particular circumſtances. How peculiarly hard muſt that woman's ſituation be, who, poſſeſſing the moſt un-adulterated paſſion, and being entirely cut off from all manner of communication with the object of her love, muſt, in obedience to an arbitrary cuſtom, linger out her days in the moſt excruciating torture—not daring to employ the means neceſſary to reſtore her peace of mind. Here ſhe pauſed—but without giving him time to reply, proceeded:—This is the caſe with me—there-fore, your generoſity will, I truſt, plead in my behalf, and ſtimulate you to pardon me, for deviating from the common path, as you are the cauſe, though perhaps never intended or deſired it.

You ſurprize me, exceedingly, madam, replied Mer-cutio; I am not conſcious of having, by any means——No, no, ſaid ſhe, interrupting him, I am convinced you never intended to inſpire me with ſuch tender ſen-timents, as thoſe I imbibed on the firſt ſight of you laſt night, and which now and ever ſince that fatal mo-ment pervade my ſoul—I ſhould be happy in a convic-tion of your having come to the entertainment, with ſuch an intention: for then I ſhould have reaſon to hope for a ſuitable return. But, if ſome happier maid has already ſecured your affections, and the avenues leading to your heart thereby eternally barred againſt me, I cannot—will not long ſurvive the diſcovery.

Mercutio, for the firſt time ſince the death of Lucin-da, found his heart powerfully aſſailed on all ſides, by

the charms of Leonora, whofe movements were fo
rapid, that he had not time to collect his forces : What
wonder then, if fhe carried her point by a coup-de-
main ? She requefted that he would accompany her
into the houfe—he complied—what man could have
refufed ?—Their love became reciprocal——mutual
careffes fucceeded the moft unequivocal proteftations
of eternal fidelity, and *********************.

Man, in the courfe of his peregrination through life,
is, and juftly, fubject to innumerable difappointments
and inquietudes, which act more or lefs powerfully, in
proportion as his fenfibility is more or lefs refined.
The fenfibility of Mercutio was of that kind which is
denominated the moft delicate, confequently, real fuf-
ferings made more lafting impreffion on his mind, than
they would probable on one lefs fufceptible : For tho'
he did not lack a degree of philofophy, and reliance
on providence, fufficient to fupport him under the
common accidents of life ; yet, like all the defcen-
dants of Adam, he had a fpark of that frailty, which, in
thofe receffes of reafon when the foul is left unguarded,
and open to the hoftile attacks of misfortune, expels
both religion and philofophy, and, by debilitating the
mental faculties, abforbs every idea of happinefs, repre-
fents every object, paft, prefent and future, in the moft
gloomy colours, and in the moft difcouraging points of
view, by which means perfons under fuch circumftances fometimes become lunatic, or raving, and too frequently have recourfe to fuicide, in order to fhun mis-

fortunes which are commonly imaginary. How remarkably kind and indulgent is Providence in cafes of
this nature : For when the mind has experienced any
uncommon fhock, there is always a counterpoife placed
within reach, fufficient to prevent the dreadful effects of
a mind furcharged with grief. This was exemplified
in the cafe before us : For had Mercutio remained at
home, a variety of objects would frequently have awakened the remembrance of Lucinda, and kept his mind
in a continual ftate of dreary folitude, if not abfolute
defpair. But by a myflerious concatenation of events,
we behold him reinftated in his former vigour and gaiety
—involuntarily engaged in an amour, which, though
apparently criminal, is not abfolutely fo ; for his intention was to repair the error he had been fuddenly
betrayed into, by an honorable marriage, as fcon as
a convenient opportunity fhould prefent.

The female confidante, before the dawning of the
day, gave Mercutio notice it was time to decamp.
Though this was an unwelcome piece of intelligence,
yet a compliance being abfolutely neceffary, they parted, with reluctance, Leonora having previoufly preffed
a very valuable ring on the finger of Mercutio, which
fhe requefted him to wear in teftimony of her unalter-
able attachment.

Having propofed to renew his vifit, on an appointed
evening, his female conductrefs efcorted him to the fpot
where fhe had met him the evening before, and on the

way, laid down a very judicious and well-conftructed plan for their future operations, and withal, pointing out the moft infallible marks whereby he might find the wicket without difficulty or danger of being difcovered. Having rewarded her honefty with a few pieces, he repaired to his lodgings, juft as the dawn of day began to appear, and went immediately to bed, where the foft balm of fleep locked up his faculties, while his countenance exhibited a type of death—his imagination being fteadily fixed on the object of his love.

About noon, his friend George waited on him, to whom Mercutio made known every particular of his nocturnal adventure——But pray inform me, faid he, if fo much may tranfpire, in what part of Venice does your fair enamoretto dwell? Indeed, replied Mercutio, I am not able to folve that queftion, though I am of opinion, I could find the houfe ; but the way to and from it is fo intricate, that it would be next to an impoffibility for me to point out the particular fpot, until I make a further difcovery, which I am determined to attempt this day. But, my dear George, I muft requeft you to keep this matter a profound fecret, becaufe I have very cogent reafons to fufpect that the young lady is of an exalted rank, and if the affair fhould inadvertently be developed, difagreeable confequences might enfue. Pardon me for giving you this (perhaps needlefs) caution, as it does not proceed from a doubt of your fidelity : but from a conviction of the tendernefs of your connections, which will fcarcely admit of the leaft

E

reserve. For, added he, I have experienced too many
proofs of your sincere attachment, to harbour the most
distant idea of your saying or doing any thing that might
prove injurious to me, with design. George assured
him he should never abuse the confidence reposed in
him, by any means, adding, that it would afford him
the highest satisfaction to see his friend completely happy.

After dinner, he sallied forth, determining to explore, by day-light, the mine which contained the sum
of all his earthly treasure. Accordingly, passing thro'
all those crooked defiles through which he had been conducted the preceding night, soon discovered the wicket, which he passed with some precipitation, and
passing two angles of the garden-wall, found himself in
a spacious street, where, running his eye along that side
of the wall which fronted the street, he perceived a con-
nection between it and a magnificent building,
which he rightly conjectured must be the house he
sought. He was confirmed in this opinion—for, passing on the opposite side of the street, he perceived two
young ladies at one of the windows, one of whom was
Leonora. She observed him, and instantly retired.

He hurried home, and having described the building,
&c. to his friend, was assured, it could be no other than
the palace of the Doge, and that his mistress must be
his daughter. This information was received with
manifest satisfaction by Mercutio, who determined
to pursue his amour in consequence.

He carried on his operations with such precaution, that he continued his nocturnal vifits for the fpace of eight months, when the effects of their illicit commerce began to appear, and to conceal it much longer, would have been a difficult tafk, if not utterly impracticable. This circumftance, which, in another fituation, would have heightened their joys into rapture, embarraffed them exceedingly : But though difficulty and danger { ftared them in the face, neither love, fortitude or invention deferted them in this emergency.

Speedy and effectual meafures being abfolutely neceffary, they devoted one whole night in deliberating what was moft proper to be done ; and after propofing and rejecting feveral plans, determined, that Mercutio fhould immediately provide for their tranfportation to England, if poffible ; if not, to fome other part of the world. In the mean time, Leonora, with the affiftance of Margaretta, her maid, fhould be fetting all things in proper train for an elopement at a minute's warning. Thefe preliminaries being fettled, he returned home, and taking his well-tried friend afide, made known the project, and earneftly folicited his affiftance.

I have a plan in my head, (faid George, after paufing fome time) which I am of opinion, if adopted, cannot fail of being fuccefsful. I have a light veffel lying at a fmall diftance from hence, which arrived but yefterday from Valona, whither fhe had been with a cargo of merchandize. Now, as the utmoft privacy is requifte,

it would be highly improper to attempt failing in any of
the veffels lying in the gulph, except this, as there is
not one bound to any port in Great-Britain: I can
have her ready in twelve hours, and will carry you
down to Ofimo in eight more, from whence you may
travel eafily over land to Naples, in a fhort time, and
remain incog. until your miftrefs can proceed with lefs
difficulty, if you think proper; if not, there are generally fhips from every part of Europe, fo that you may
fail for England when you pleafe.   Now, what do you
think of my plan? Why, I think, faid Mercutio,
nothing could have been fo fortunate, and it fhall be
put in execution this night, if agreeable to you.   The
fooner the better, faid he, for it is hardly known that
the veffel has returned, and if we can fail early in the
night, I can replace her in her prefent fituation by fun-
rife to-morrow at fartheft, and fhall never be miffed.
Thefe reafons appearing perfectly fatisfactory, he took
leave in order to make the neceffary preparations for
his departure.   In the afternoon, they went on board,
in order to fhow the fervants where to carry the baggage, as foon as it was dark, while Mercutio conducted Leonora.   After taking a view of the veffel, and
learning the neareft way to it, they returned to George's
houfe, and by the time they had taken a flight refrefh-
ment it was dufk. George, offered it as his opinion,
that it would be moft proper to depart without taking
a formal leave of the family, adding, that after matters
were fettled, and they arrived in England, he might write
to his uncle, and inform him of the reafon of his abrupt

departure. This was agreed to, and Mercutio sat out, to pay his last visit at the Doge's, while his servants conveyed the baggage on board, and George with his little crew, got up the anchor, and unfurled the sails, so that there might be no delay.

Mercutio found his mistress ready and willing to depart, so that they soon sallied out at the wicket, and bidding an eternal, though silent farewell to the Doge, proceeded towards the water side : The faithful Margaretta bearing a large bundle of wearing apparel, and Mercutio an ebony box, crammed with ducats, which Leonora put into his hands, just as they were leaving the house, though he was ignorant of its contents until after their arrival at Naples.—They embarked safely, having a fine breeze from the westward, and a strong current setting outward, anchored at Osimo in six hours.

It happened very fortunate for our adventurers, that George had an intimate friend there, who at that time lay under particular obligations to him. As soon as they dropped anchor, George went on shore, and repaired immediately to the house of his friend, and informed him, that there was a gentleman and his wife on board his vessel, wishing to proceed to Naples, and for particular reasons, to perform their journey as privately as possible, and requested him to procure a convenient vehicle to transport them. Here, said he, are thirty ducats—be faithful—be diligent. This is but a trifling earnest of what I will do further for you. The gentle-

man will correspond with me during his stay at Naples
—you will forward our letters with care, secrecy and
expedition.   His friend assured him he was happy in
being charged with this commission, as it would afford
him an opportunity of demonstrating his gratitude for
the many favours he had already received   Well,
said George, I rely on your word ; now come with me
and conduct them to your house, for I want to sail immediately—I expect to see you again in a few days—
in the mean time let nothing extort this secret from you.

George returned on board, and informed his departing friend the substance of his negociation : Then taking
an affectionate farewell, those adventurers landed, and
followed their new host ; while George spread the canvas to the wind, which at that time had veered round
several points in his favour, so that before the day
dawned he had remoored and got home to his own
house—having performed a trip of more than forty-
six leagues, in something less than ten hours and a half.

Proper apartments being assigned for the reception of
our adventurers, they retired to rest, whilst the vigilant
host went in search of a carriage to convey them to
Naples, the ensuing day.   Having succeeded to his
wish, he returned, and informed his guests, who were
then up, and taking chocolate with his wife, a woman
of good sense, who informed Leonora, that she had a
sister, a widow, in Naples, an approved and experienced
midwife, that kept a commodious house fitted for the

reception of ladies in her fituation, where they might be accommodated with every thing neceffary as long as fhe pleafed to remain. This was an agreeable piece of information ; and her hufband, in order to fulfil his engagements with George; in the fulleft extent, made a tender of his fervice to accompany them to his fifter in-law's, and negociate the whole bufinefs for them immediately on their arrival. This propofal was accepted with joy, as it feemed exactly adapted to their circumftances ; for 'twould have been madnefs to have taken Leonora to fea, except in a cafe of the moft preffing neceffity.

They ftarted next morning with the firft light, and arrived at the place of their deftination on the fourth day about fun-fet. When they were within two leagues of Naples, their hoft rode forward to provide for their reception, which having accomplifhed, he met the carriage about half a mile from the city, where they alighted and walked to their lodgings. They received a very cordial welcome from the miftrefs of the houfe, who was a genteel affable perfon. An elegant fupper was ferved up, of which our young travellers eat hearty ; and at an early hour were conducted to proper apartments for repofe.

The next morning, Mercutio wrote to his friend George, to inform him of their fafe arrival, and requefted him to write as fpeedily as poffible, as Leonora was anxious to hear how matters were conducted at Venice, in confequence of her elopement—well knowing her father's impetuous temper would, in the firft torrent of his rage, bear down all before it. This letter he delivered to his generous hoft, accompanied by a purfe of ducats, which, for fome time he ftrenuoufly refufed; but on Mercutio's declaring, he fhould not look on him as his friend, if he did not accept it, with reluctance complied, faying, heaven knows, I neither wifhed or expected any reward for the trifling pains I have taken to ferve you—you may reft affured, I would not have done and promifed what I have on any other confideration, but that of ferving my friend, who informed me, is deeply interefted in what concerns your welfare. He then departed, with a promife to forward all letters that came under his care, to and from him, with the greateft fecrecy and difpatch.

In five days, Mercutio had the inexpreffible fatisfaction of receiving the following letter from George, by the hand of his late friendly hoft :—

"My dear friend,

"I received yours by the bearer, who is faithful and diligent, and am happy to hear of your being accommodated fo much to your fatisfaction. You wifh to know the confequence of your departure—I will tell you : I arrived here fafely, before day, the next morning after I parted with you. All things remained quiet that day——but there was not a crevice in Venice left unfearched by the enfuing evening. The fuccefs, attending the fearch you are acquainted with. The Doge finding his endeavors to recover his daughter fruitlefs, caufed ftrict enquiry to be made, whether any veffel had failed that night, or fince, and was informed that a certain fwift-failing floop had weighed, and ftood out to fea early in the morning, but her deftination could not be afcertained. He naturally concluded fhe was on board the floop. A young gentleman, a native of France, had left his lodgings, the houfe of an eminent merchant which ftood in the fame ftreet where the Doge's palace ftands, where he had refided for feveral months, that very evening. It feems he had contracted an intimacy with his landlord's daughter, the effects of which began to appear ; and although fhe loved him to diftraction, and was willing to fuffer any thing rather than a feparation, yet the unfeeling villain abfconded privately, and probably failed in the floop, leaving the diftreffed creature to a fate, which makes me fhudder at the bare recital. The Doge obtained information of a perfon of this defcription having eloped, gave peremptory orders to have the merchant and his whole family inftantly feized and brought before him, concluding that their lodger had carried off his daughter, and they of courfe acceffary : For as yet his feducing the merchant's daughter was not fufpected. In vain the Doge endeavoured to extort confeffion from each of them apart, they perfifted in their innocence : He, therefore, commanded them to be feparately confined till next morning, threatning them with the rack if they fhould ftill

perfift.   The next day it was the fame, but their affeverations of innocence ferved only to enrage the Doge.
He ordered the inftruments of torture to be brought
into his prefence.   The merchant's daughter falling on
her knees deplored the Doge to defer the dreadful punifhment for a few minutes, while fhe difclofed the fecrets
of her foul, of which her parents were ignorant. With
a look of indignation he ordered her to proceed. Tho'
my dear parents and my wretched felf ftand as crimi-
nals in your prefence, my lord, yet I truft I fhall be
able to convince you of our innocence; yet in fo
doing, I muft publifh my own fhame.   If M. de Gar-
delle has robbed Venice of fo great a treafure as my
lord's daughter, his treachery to me, and ingratitude
to my parents, muft forever acquit us of having been
either acceffaries or principals in the crime.   For,
know, my lord, the faithlefs wretch had previoufly
effected the deftruction of the haplefs woman who now
addreffes you :—In a fatal hour I yielded to his falfe
promifes, and by that means rendered myfelf an object
of contempt.   It is probable, by his artifice, he has
found means to feduce your daughter, and, knowing
my fituation, perfuaded her to accompany him to
France, where it is likely, when fated with her company, he will abandon her as he has me, to all the horrors of infamy and defpair !—Oh! my unhappy parents!
Pardon your wretched daughter—who cannot, will not
furvive the publication of her difgrace !——As fhe
pronounced thefe words, fhe, to the aftonifhment of all
prefent, plunged a poignant in her breaft, and expired

inftantly. Such a horrid fcene, could not fail to im-
prefs the mind of the Doge and thofe of the fpectators,
with a ftrong conviction of the fincerity of her confeffion,
as well as of the innocence of her parents. The Doge
retired with manifeft marks of forrow and confufion,
and gave immediate orders for the liberation of the unhappy parents, who continued bathing the body of
their dear, unfortunate child with tears ! The next
day, the Doge fent for them, and was clofeted with
them for the fpace of three hours. The refult of their
conference has not yet tranfpired : but the merchant,
who is a native of Spain, with the remains of his family, embarked this morning for Valencia.

" Since this unhappy affair happened, there has been
very little faid about it, as the Venetians feem willing
to confign the remembrance of fuch a lamentable cata-
ftrophe to eternal oblivion. Let me intreat you to remain as quiet as poffible, during your ftay at Naples ;
and as foon as circumftances will admit, to take fhip-
ping for England. I informed my uncle the caufe of
your abrupt departure ; concealing, however, my fhare
in the enterprize : He is well pleafed at your efcape,
and defires me to prefent his refpects to you, together
with his fincere wifhes for your future welfare.——
Continue to write every opportunity, and reft affured
of my being, and remaining your fincere friend,

" GEORGE WRIGHT."

Mercutio, in confequence of the preceding information, refolved, as foon as Leonora was able to ftir about
after her confinement, to fail for England.

At length, the much defired period arrived—when
fhe was fafely delivered of a beautiful boy, to the no
fmall fatisfaction of our hero and his lovely companion.
Leonora being diligently attended by her kind hoftefs,
and the faithful Magaretta, was foon in a fituation to
undertake the intended voyage. Her fon, healthful
and vigorous, grew exceedingly faft, and his father's
features were ftrikingly depicted in his face, which circumftance gave birth to the moft pleafing reflections in
the minds of his parents.

Mercutio began immediately to make diligent enquiry for an Englifh fhip ; and finding one bound for Liverpool, bargained with the commander, whofe name
was Nicholfon, for his paffage. The fhip waited for
nothing but a fair wind, therefore, he was as expeditious as poffible, in providing neceffaries for the
voyage, and conveying his baggage on board. Having
arranged all his affairs in ample order, nothing remained to be done, but to fatisfy his hoftefs, and write a
farewell epiftle to his friend George. They devoted
the laft evening to mirth and hilarity ; our hero having previoufly difcharg'd his reckoning with two hundred ducats. Juft as they were fitting down to fupper, they were furpriz'd by the appearance of George
and his friend. Mutual falutations paft, George in-

formed them the caufe of his journey as follows :——
" About three days ago, I was informed by a Venetian gentleman, a friend of the Doge's, that the Doge
of Naples had fent a very preffing invitation to the Doge
of Venice, to honour him with a vifit, which, in confideration of the one he received from him when you
were there, as well as the ftrict amity exifting between
them, he had accepted, and is expected in Naples this
evening.   I was afraid to commit this piece of intelligence to paper, and therefore fet out as foon as I poffibly could, in order to let you know your danger : For
a difcovery now, might be attended with dreadful confequences."—My ineftimable friend, replied Mercutio,
how fhall I ever make you a fuitable return for your
difinterefted exertions in my favour? Unadulterated
friendfhip is all you hold worthy your acceptance, and
it fhall be my chief care, to preferve that inviolate and
undiminifhed.   We are, my dear George, to embark
for Liverpool to-morrow morning—I have every thing
on board, and if the wind fhould prove favorable, the
fhip will fail immediately, fo that if heaven permits,
we fhall foon be on the Britifh fhore ; and, probably,
the firft letter you receive from me will inform you of
the celebration of our happy union. May heaven
grant you a fafe, and agreeable paffage, returned George.

At a very late hour they retired to reft, and before
the dawn of day, were all affembled in the common
apartment, where they reiterated their former profeffions of eternal friendfhip. Our voyagers taking

F

an affectionate leave of their hostess, set out, accompanied by George and his friend. The anchor was weighing by the time they got on board, and George, having seen them safe through the whole of this dangerous enterprize, wished them a prosperous voyage, and returned to the shore..

Our hero was as happy at the commencement of this voyage, as the nature of the circumstances would permit : Leonora too, promised herself the most perfect felicity in the endearing company of her beloved Mercutio, and with the enchanting prattle of the dear pledge of their mutual affection. Mercutio had previously dispatched a packet to England, to inform his friends of the time of his intended departure from Naples, and in the letter to his mother, he signified his intention of bringing with him a Venetian lady, whom he intended to make his wife, with the approbation of his friends, immediately on his arrival in London. But it is the uncontrolable will of heaven, that man, when he forgets his origin, and looks up with confidence to supreme felicity as already within his grasp, should experience the chastifing rod of affliction, in order to bring him to a sense of his duty—to acknowledge his own imbecility and the omnipotence of that Being, from whom all happiness, whether in heaven or on earth, must flow ; and to whom all thanks are necessarily due. A striking instance of this was exhibited in the case before us. Mercutio conceived that nothing could intervene to blast the flattering prospect which had just engaged his attention; but which was on the eve of difappearing: The fatal moment was faſt approaching, in which all his imaginary joys were to vaniſh, like the fleeting meteor: The cloud was already collected, and fufpending over his head, which was ſhortly to burſt and involve him in miſery. How vain! how trifling! in the view of Omnipotence, are the purſuits of ſhort fighted mortals;—ever anxious to ſecure happineſs which ſhall be permanent, our imagination is eternally on the wing; our invention is tortured for ſchemes to ſecure the glittering phantom, and we madly reject the ſubſtance, which thro' life, is conſtantly within our reach; and ignorantly purſue a ſhadow, which we never can—never will overtake.

They had juſt weather'd Comin, on the Iſle of Sardinia, when a moſt tremendous hurricane from the N. W. accompanied with an irreſiſtable current ſetting out of the gulph of Lyons, and violently paſſing between Minorca and Sardinia, drove them, in ſpite of their ſkill and induſtry, into the Streights of Meſſina. The day was juſt cloſing when they doubled the cape, which tended to aggravate the horror of the ſcene which immediately ſucceeded. The awful burſts of thunder, and ſtreams of livid lightning, together with dreadful ſqualls of hail, rain, and wind, ſeemed to threaten a final diſſolution. The whole univerſe appeared in violent convulſions, and the ſhip was hurled about like an egg-ſhell in this elemental conflict, which none but the moſt inſenſible being, could have beheld without horror. To adminifter comfort to Leonora was the whole bufinefs of Mercutio, during the ftorm, and it was with much difficulty he preferved her from fainting.

About day light, however, it pleas'd that God in whofe hand the whole univerfe is but as a grain of fand, to quell the fury of the unfathomable deep—to rebuke the winds; and immediately all was hufh'd into profund tranquillity. The clouds difpers'd—the blue concave appear'd in its native fplendor, and the beams of that glorious diffufer of light and heat, conveyed new vigor to the benumbed limbs of the fatigued mariners, and cheerfulnefs once more reigned throughout the whole.

As foon as the ftorm fubfided, captain Nicholfon ordered all hands to appear on the quarter deck, when both feamen and paffengers bent, in lowly reverence, to that all merciful Being, whofe affiftance is ever at hand, to relieve and fupport his unworthy creatures, and offered up the acceptable facrifice of grateful hearts, in the moft unfeigned thanks for his divine protection during the ftorm, without which they muft inevitably have perifhed. This done, they began to repair their fhattered fails and rigging, which had fuffered much in the hurricane. Though they were much rejoiced with their late deliverance, their fatisfaction was confiderably damped, when the captain found that they were within a few leagues of Malta, and lefs of the coaft of

Barbary ; and, as the wind ſtill blew freſh from the N.
W. it would be exceedingly difficult to keep off the
coaſt ; confequently, they would be in continual danger
of the rovers, until they made the Streights of Gi-
braltar. They inſtantly braced up, and laid the ſhip
as cloſe to the wind as poſſible, ſtood away for the
South point of Sicily. They had failed only three
hours in this direction, when the captain, from the main
topmaſt head, difcovered a corfair, at the diſtance of
about three leagues and a half, bearing down on them.
Capt. Nicholſon immediately ſhifted his courſe, in
hopes of making Puzoli, before the pirate could reach
them ; but in this he was unfortunately difappointed ;
though it is very probable, he might have ſucceded,
had his veſſel been in as good failing order, as ſhe was
before the late ſtorm ; but it was impracticable in the
prefent ſhattered condition to efcape—the pirates
gained on them every moment.

When the captain found all his endeavours to efcape
fruitleſs, he told Mercutio, that their liberty, property,
and perhaps lives, depended on their courage and ac-
tivity : Therefore, added he, I expect you will lend me
all the aſſiſtance in your power. There are three guns
on board, which I will load with grape, and bring
them to bear in an oblique direction : I have fixteen
hands befides myfelf, and you with your two fervants
will make twenty ;—we have fmall arms plenty, with
which we muſt endeavour to prevent them from board-
ing us :—For my part, I am determined never to fur-

render while I have a living man, or a load of ammu-
nition on board. We will, continued he, flee from
them as fast as we can, as well to gain time to arrange
matters, as to amuse and fatigue them—and when they
get within reach of our guns, suddenly tack and pour in
a volley, which, perhaps, will throw them into disorder,
and if their number and metal does not exceed ours,
decide the matter in our favor.

Mercutio assured him, that all the assistance in his
power should be devoted to his service, and they imme-
mediately made the necessary dispositions for the event.
The pirate, in the mean time, was not idle, but bore
down upon them with crouded sails and oars ; and in
a short time hailed captain Nicholson, and ordered him,
if he wished to experience any mercy, to bring too
immediately, and strike his colours. The captain
having all things in readiness, clapt his helm a-lee, and
was about in an instant ; then poured in a well-directed
fire, which killed four of the Turks and wounded two Christian slaves, who were chained to the oar.
This sudden, unexpected volley, and the execution
performed by it, disconcerted the pirates considerably,
but being thirty in number, besides eight Christians at
the oar, they returned the fire vigorously, and dropping
astern, discharged six double fortified fours into the
cabin windows, by which, the unfortunate Leonora,
her son, and Margaretta, were at the same moment, sent
into eternity !—The galley then came along side, and
the commander levelling his piece at the brave captain

Nicholfon, fhot him through the heart. Mercutio continued the conflict, with great firmnefs and courage.
The galley having grappled the fhip, the infidels immediately attempted to board her; but were bravely
repulfed—Mercutio, jumping into the mizen chains,
cut off, with his hanger, the arms of two Turks, who
fell overboard and were drowned. The pirates then
made a feint of falling off; but juſt as our hero was
ſtepping out of the chains, he received a ball in his
right knee, which laid him proſtrate on the quarter
deck. The pirates immediately grappled again, and
without much refiſtance, boarded the fhip, as there
were only two men left unwounded. Captain Nicholfon, his two mates, the carpenter, Mercutio's two
fervants, and five foremaſt men were killed; and Mercutio, the boatſwain, cook, cabin-boy, and three ſailors
wounded. The lofs on the part of the Turks, was
twelve killed, exclufive of four ſlaves, and three
wounded.

Mercutio's wound bled amazingly, by which means
he became infenfible, and remained in that fituation till
the pirates, perceiving fome figns of life, and judging
by his habit, that he was a perfon of diſtinction, had
conveyed him on board the galley, and confined him to
a ring-bolt, on his back. 'Twas in this unhappy fituation he became fenfible, when, making an effort to
rife, he found himfelf chained hand and foot!—But
what words can defcribe the intolerable anguiſh
of his foul, when he was informed, by one of his

fellow-captives, of the dreadful fate of the beauteous Leonora and her lovely infant! Had he not been chained faſt to the deck, it is more than probable, that, in the midſt of deſpair, he would have leaped overboard; but finding it impoſſible to move out of the ſpot, he gave himſelf up to immoderate grief! and formed the deſperate reſolution of taking no food, in order, as he expreſſed it, to end his life and miſeries as quick as poſſible.

The wound he had received having never been attended, grew very painful; and being overheated in the action, he had caught a violent cold, which brought on an intermittent fever, ſo that at the time the galley arrived at Algiers, he was actually delirious. The renegado who commanded, was a Spaniard, who judging Mercutio a perſon of quality, had him taken to his own houſe, and procured an eminent phyſician, who applied ſuch healing medicines, that in about one month he was reinſtated in his health; but ſtill remained diſconſolate for his beloved Leonora and darling ſon.

The renegado, perceiving the health of Mercutio reſtored, aſked him ſeveral queſtions relative to his country and connexions, and whether he had any expectation of being ranſomed. Mercutio anſwered, that if a letter could be conveyed ſafely to London, he was ſure of being ranſomed. This was granted, and he diſpatched one letter to his father, and another to his friend George Wright.

The renegado demanded three hundred crowns for his ranfom ; and as he had loft feveral of his men in the late engagement, he took our hero and three of his fellow captives on board his own galley, where they were conftrained to row night and day, chained to the thwart they fat on. They had no occafion to per-form voluntary abftinence ; for their food was of the coarfeft kind, and the quantities fo fmall as to be but barely fufficient to fupport them in a life of wretched bondage. This cruel flavery bore much heavier on Mercutio than his companions in diftrefs, having never been accuftomed to hardfhips. His hands were foon ftript of fkin, yet his mercilefs commanders compel-led him to labour, though the blood ran in ftreams down the handle of the oar.—He who 'till then, had been clothed with the fineft production of the loom, had no other covering than a frock and drawers of the coarfeft canvas, without fhoes or ftockings. His feet began to fwell and grow exceedingly pain-ful. Three months had elapfed without any news arriving from England or Venice, all hands having been preffed in the Downs out of the veffel that had failed to England ; and the other having foundered off Minorca, and all on board perifhed : However, he obtained leave to write once more to Venice, and, in a·bout fix weeks, received a letter from his friend George, wherein he affured him he fhould have the money in fifteen days without fail.

The money arrived at the appointed time, with three
hundred crowns more than he had requested, to furnish
him with clothes and other necessaries ; and an
invitation, to come and reside in Venice for some
time. Our hero would willingly have waved going
there, well knowing that the very sight of the city would be a dagger to his soul ; yet, the regard he
had for his friend, and the great and many obligations he lay under, silenced every objection that presented itself, and decided the matter quickly. He
paid the renegado the sum demanded for his own ran-
som, and two hundred crowns for his three companions
in slavery, who, with himself were immediately liberat-
ted. He gave the three poor fellows ten crowns each,
and told them to make the best of their way home ;
but they finding him going to Venice ; begged permission to sail on board the same ship, as they had no
chance of getting their passage to England, and added,
that, when he was gone, the Turks might seize and
enslave them again. This he complied with, and they
all embarked on board the ship in which George had
sent the money, and arrived at Venice in a short time.

Our hero having taken leave of these poor fellows,
who expressed their gratitude to him in the most fervent
manner, went to see his well tried friend; whom he
found in health, but not quite so cheerful as formerly, having just returned from the funeral of his uncle
and aunt, who both expired in one day. He was received, however, with unaffected kindness, which he

experienced for the fpace of fix weeks, the time he remained in Venice ; and, having pretty well recruited his health and fpirits, he refolved to embark for England on board the firft fhip he could find bound thither. George endeavoured to diffuade him from his purpofe, by reprefenting to him the danger of being captured by the French privateers ; that nation having entered into an alliance with the States of America : Who had thrown off the Hanoverian yoke, and declared themfelves Independent ; and, under the aufpices of a gentleman of Virginia, (George Wafhington) who had given indubitable proofs of his bravery and fkill in tactics, in former wars between France and England, were bravely ftruggling againft the defpotic arms of Great-Britain, in fupport of the indefeafible Rights of Man..

Mercutio, however, was not to be diverted from undertaking, his intended voyage : Difconfolate for the lofs of Leonora, and weary of the repeated viciffitudes of his adverfe fate, he refolved to attempt a paffage to England at all events.

George finding it to no purpofe to perfift, urged the matter no further ; but procured a veffel, and furnifhed him with a fum of money, more than fufficient to defray every expence. In a fhort time he was ready to embark, and having taken leave of his kind friends, with the moft grateful acknowledgment for all paft favors, and promifing to remit the money George had

ſo freely advanced for his ranſom, &c. by the firſt opportunity after-his arrival in London, once more bid
adieu to Venice.

Fortune favoured them with proſperous gales and
pleaſant weather ; and in a few days, they were imper-
ceptibly waſted within ſight of the Lizard.   Mercutio,
for the firſt time, ſince his redemption from captivity,
became cheerful.   He experienced that kind of ſatis-
faction, which the hopleſs mariner, who, having been
deprived the ſight of land or ſunſhine for many days,
and all the time threatened by the devouring waves, to
be buried in the bowels of the deep, is ſuddenly waſted
into the deſired haven.

They arrived, and moored off Deal without an accident. Mercutio propoſed hiring a poſt-chaiſe, and to ſet
out for London the next morning.   But alas ! Fortune,
that fickle goddeſs, had raiſed her foot with a deſign to
give him another kick.   Preſs-warrants were out for
raiſing ten thouſand ſeamen ; in conſequence of which,
a lieutenant and forty ſeamen boarded the ſhip, about
midnight ; and, ſlipping down between decks, made
prize of the whole crew, and among the reſt, Mercutio.

Reſiſtance would have been as vain as it was impracticable, they therefore made a virtue of neceſſity,
and ſubmitted to be conveyed on board the Otter, (a
tender) where they remained for ſome days, and then
put on board the Iſis, of 50 guns, at Spithead.   They
were welcomed on board with three cheers from the

whole crew. The lieutenant who had preſſed them, caufed plenty of grog to be diſtributed among the new hands: This done, he ordered the boatſwain's mate to bring them aft, where he read over the articles of war; after which, he entertained them with the following eloquent harrangue:

"Ship-mates and brother ſailors!—But I ſpeak chiefly to you that's come aboard laſt. Tho' you are prefs'd, you needn't think you're kidnapped:—No, damme, boys—you have liberty to enter your names in the ſhip's books, and receive the bounty.——Now, ſince you're aboard, and muſt ſtay whether you will or not, you may as well conſent to enter——The king muſt have ſailors to deſtroy them d—n'd French b—gg—rs that's combined with the rebels d'ye fee; and if we don't kill 'em, take 'em, ſink 'em, make 'em run away, d—n my eyes, boys.——Come, my boys, you that's a mind to enter, come aft, and give your name to the purfer—he's as honeſt a fellow as ever the devil got— he'll give you the bounty and plenty of grog, by G—d, —Huzza! God ſave the king!—Huzza!"

The major part of the preſſed men accepted this po- lite invitation, while he continued to diſplay his rhetori- cal powers:—"Come, my brave meſs-mates, now is the time to EXTINGUISH yourſelves in OFFENCE of your king and country——There an't a man in England but muſt turn out now, d—n me, either by ſea or land; and, for my part, I'd rather be an under-turnkey in hell, than a SOGER, d—n me if I had'nt."

G

This animating oration had a great effect on the tar-
pawlings ; for as he very juftly obferved, there they
were, and there they were like to remain, confequently, might as well comply as not—fo they generally
took his advice. Adverfe as Mercutio's fate appeared,
he did not abfolutely defpair of procuring his liberty, if
he could gain accefs to the commander ; but found, on
enquiry, that he was on fhore.   Finding no officer on
board fuperior to this loquacious fon of Neptune, he
refolved to folicit his affiftance in remitting a letter to
London.   Having executed this refolve, this patriotic
officer gave him the following anfwer :—" I'll tell you
what, mefs-mate, you may write a letter to Lunnan,
but I'm d—'d if I think it will be of any fervice to you.
However, if you think it will do you any good, as you
have the look of a clever fellow, I'll fpeak to the purfer for pen, ink and paper for you ; and when I go
afhore to night, I'll clap it in the poft-office. But God
knows when or where we fhall fail—we may fail to-
morrow, and mayhap we may'nt this month, d'ye fee."
Mercutio thanked him for his civility, and told him he
would fatisfy him for his trouble.   He went down to
the purfer, and foon returned with a quire of paper, an
inkftand, and a parcel of pens ; and beckoning to him,
in a vociferous tone, faid, " Mefs-mate, come down
into my cabin, and there you may write as much as
you pleafe—here's pen, ink, and paper enough to fet
the whole world in an uproar——Old Singe-the-Devil,
d—n his old frofty face, charged me four fhillin for this
roll of paper : He never thinks he has enough for any

thing——I'd rather be a pu.
he cheats the failors, the officers, .

Our hero put his hand in his pocket, and pulling
ten dollars, prefented them to the lieutenant, which he
received with much apparent fatisfaction, faying, at the
fame time—" By G—d, meffmate, you're the heartieft
fellow I've met this war. The king, God blefs him,
owes me five hundred guineas ; but I think money
d—n'd fcarce with him as well as us. The admiral
fays we fhall all be paid off when we come home ; but
d—n me if I believe him, d'ye fee."

Our hero paid very little attention to what he faid,
but fat down on a cheft, and wrote a very preffing letter to his father, informing him of the defperate circumftances under which he lay, and earneftly requefting him to employ all poffible means to obtain his releafe. Having delivered the letter to his friend the
lieutenant, he grew cheerful, and began to cherifh the
hope of being yet reftored to his friends, without being
forced to fea again. But Providence, it feems, had
otherwife decreed. The next morning, very early,
orders came on board, for the Ifis, with two frigates,
and fome tranfports, to weigh, and fail the next tide.
Their deftination was to fome part of the Continent ;
but as the fpecial orders were fealed, and not to be
opened till they had got into a certain degree of latitude,
the particular port was unknown.

rs who had been on shore,
er the sailing orders, and Mer-
ication, by letter (through his friend
eutenant) for a discharge—but without effect :
in vain he represented the sufferings he had endured in
Algiers, from whence he had been so lately redeemed
—he was deaf to his entreaties : All the consolation he received, was, that if he behaved well, he might
make his fortune before the war was over.

Finding all his efforts defeated, he consigned himself
to his fate. His countenance became gloomy and
thoughtful ; and had he remained long in that state, it
is more than probable, he would have degenerated into a most unsocial being—so, true it is, that the sweetest
temper may be soured by frequent repulses and disap-
pointments.

The necessary preparations being made, the anchor was weighed ; the sails extended to the expanding
gale ; and with drums beating, trumpets sounding,
colours flying, and every other demonstration of naval
joy, they took their departure.

Satisfaction appeared conspicuous on every countenance on board, except that of Mercutio's, which was
impressed with marks of the deepest melancholy. His
uneasiness was taken notice of by several of the officers
as well as the seamen, particularly by the first lieutenant, who brought on board the orders for sailing ; but

had never taken notice of Mercutio till they had been a full week at sea. This gentleman obferving him in a penfive attitude one day, at the fame time remarking, that he had not the leaft appearance of a feaman; enquired of the fecond lieutenant who he was, and from whence he came.

Being informed of this, and that he had been lately releafed from the Algerines, he was impatient to have fome difcourfe with a perfon of fo fingular a defcription. He wrote a billet, and fent it by the cabin-boy, requefting a fhort interview. Our hero, after perufing the billet, ordered the boy to conduct him to the perfon who had fent him: He followed, neither knowing nor caring who it was that defired the interview. On entering the cabin he faluted the lieutenant with a very low bow, who inftantly arofe, and taking our hero by the hand, very politely returned the falute. But what words can paint the amazement and joy of Mercutio, when in the features of the lieutenant he recognifed thofe of his beloved friend Charles, Lucinda's brother! Charles inftantly recollected his features—and rufhing into each others arms, they embraced with mutual tranfport, without uttering a fyllable: The fudden fhock of joy having fhackled their organs of fpeech for feveral minutes.

Mercutio firft recovering his fpeech faid, My dear Charles, my tongue would but difcover its impotence in attempting to defcribe the pleafing fenfations which pervade my foul, on this occafion—to meet a friend

so much esteemed, after so long and painful a separa-
ration, is a happiness so unexpected, that my weak
frame, fatigued and emaciated, with trouble, disappointment, and melancholy, is almost unable to sustain
the sudden shock, which, like the swift winged,
livid lightning, has penetrated the very centre of my
soul—stunned my whole fabric—and unhinged all my
senses. But tell me, what good genii sent you here, to
administer the balm of consolation to my distracted soul?
My beloved, respected friend, replied Charles, the supe-
rior pleasure which this happy interview affords me,
would have been incapable of augmentation, had
it not been damped by your hint of " trouble, disappointment, and melancholy," which your countenance
too clearly demonstrates to have been your companions.
What dreadful reverse of fortune can have destroy-
ed the peace of my friend ? If there is any thing within the compass of my power that will, in the smallest
degree, contribute to your ease or satisfaction, only-
mention it : Command my purse—enjoin me to
any thing I am capable of, and you shall see with
what willingness I will exert all my powers to restore
your peace of mind,

Mercutio, after making him such an answer as his
unbounded, disinterested offers merited, related the
whole of his adventures, from the time they parted
last, in London, till they met on board the Isis: concealing, however, his amour with Leonora,

Charles generoufly fympathized with him in all his misfortunes, promifed to render him all the fervice in his power, and to reprefent his cafe to the captain, who, notwithftanding his profeffion, was a gentleman of the niceft feelings, and moft diftinguifhed merit ; and, added he, if the fleet is detained on the American coaft, I think I have influence enough with him to procure your difchage, and you can fail from New-York to England at any time, as packets are conftantly going and coming. Mercutio made him a genteel acknowledgment for his intended favours ; but declared, that fince fortune had brought them together once more, he was determined to accompany him through the whole courfe of the expedition.

- Charles expreffed the higheft fatisfaction at this declaration, and protefted that no event could have happened, that could give him equal pleafure.—Mercutio then defired to be informed of his friend's reafon for making choice of a fea-faring life, together with a general narrative of his tranfactions during their long feparation. I fhall with pleafure gratify your curiofity in that point, replied Charles, but muft beg leave to wave it for the prefent, and filling a glafs of wine, prefented it to Mercutio, faying, Come, my friend, you muft endeavour to confign the remembrance of your late misfortunes over to eternal oblivion—you are now among as lively a fet of fellows as the world can produce :—They hope every thing—fear nothing—and drink punch, grog and phlip, like fo many fifhes.

Having taken a cheerful glafs, they went upon deck, when Charles, taking him by the hand, prefented him to the captain as his particular friend ; and, in a few words, informed him of the moft interefting parts of his adventures. The captain congratulated our hero on his releafe from the infidels, and at the fame time lamented the neceffity of preffing men indifcriminately : He concluded, with promifing him a total exemption from all manner of duty while he continued on board ; together with permiffion to return to England by the firft opportunity, and ample protection from all prefs-gangs during the war.

From that time Charles and Mercutio eat, drank, and flept together ; the officers vied with each other in a genteel treatment to him, and the captain became his firm friend.   Thefe fortunate circumftances produced the moft agreeable change in his countenance and converfation. One fine evening, when the furface of the immenfe ocean, calm and ferene, reflected the glittering rays of that glorious luminary, the fun, with redoubled fplendor, Mercutio, with his friend was furveying and admiring the liquid green which every where furrounded them, boundlefs ! reiterated his requeft. " Mercutio," faid Charles, " I fhould ill deferve the tender, the honorable appellation of friend, if I was capable of refufing fo trifling a gratification ; and though you will reap no pleafure in t'il information, you will at leaft confefs you are not the only perfon expofed to the frowns of fortune ; for fince you fet out on your travels, I have experienced many hard strokes myself.

"Some time after your departure, Augustus Davenport, son of Sir Edward Davenport, of Oxfordshire, having seen my sister Charlotte, at my uncle's seat, which lies contiguous to Sir Edward's, where she was on a visit, came to London, and resided with his brother in-law, Sir Benjamin Godfrey. As his journey to the metropolis, was undertaken with a view of setting on foot an hymeneal treaty between him and my sister, he engaged Sir. Benjamin, (knowing the great friendship existing between him and my father) to introduce him, and assist in the course of the negociation with his recommendation and advice.—He was shortly permitted to pay his addresses to Charlotte——When matters were nearly ripe, Augustus took leave for some time.———He returned, accompanied by his father and—a sister——That sister !—Oh Mercutio ! do not suppose yourself unfortunate !———But I'll proceed : The marriage contract being sanctioned with the approbation of all parties, they were married, to the great satisfaction of both families.

"After staying six weeks in town, Sir Edward proposed returning to his country seat ; and, as Augustus after tarrying a while at his father's, intended to take his wife to a seat which Sir Edward had lately purchased and promised to give him whenever he should enter the bands of wedlock, the old knight re-

quefted, or rather infifted, that I fhould accompany
them thither. I acquiefced, being prompted by more
powerful motives than thofe produced by his invitation.

"We fat out, all on horfe-back, and had a very
agreeable ride to Sir Edward's, who treated us nobly,
for the fpace of one month, at the end of which, Au-
guftus prepared to go to his own feat. I, as well as his
fifter, accompanied them.   But, now, Mercutio, your
repeated misfortunes, though great, will quickly difappear, when you hear the fequel——I might almoft
fay with the Ghoft of Hamlet : " I can a tale unfold,
" whofe lighteft word will harrow up thy foul ! Freeze
" thy young blood ! Make thy knotty and combined
" locks to part, and each particular hair to ftand an
" end, like quills upon the fretful porcupine !"

"This daughter of Sir Edward was, I believe, a
model of beauty and apparent innocence. She poffeffed every accomplifhment neceffary to render a
woman lovely, and the undivided poffeffion of her, a
peculiar bleffing. I have frequently when in her company, contemplated on her perfections with amazement : And, I verily believe, if any man had told me
then, of the fatal change which has fince taken place in
her, I fhould have been ready to run him through.
This enchanting paragon, without intention, or even
fufpicion, eftablifhed fo abfolute a dominion over
my foul, that the very thought of parting with her,
was as daggers to my heart !—I addreffed her on the

subject—succeeded to my wish—and, we were married: But ah! what bitter reflections does the remembrance of that cursed union awaken in my soul! One year I lived with her in so great a degree of felicity, that I would not have exchanged my situation for all the riches of the East.

"She wished to visit her friends at Oxfordshire—I consented; for what could I refuse to her whose breast was the repository of my soul?—We found Sir Edward in good health; and after staying a few days, proceeded to the feat of Augustus, where we arrived just as Charlotte had made her first appearance at church after the birth of a beautiful boy.

"While we remained there, all the neighbouring gentry for several miles round, came to congratulate the young couple on the birth of an heir. Among those who appeared the most assiduous, was Charles Howard, son to a noble Earl, who I afterwards found, had been acquainted with Louisa Davenport, from her infancy, but had not seen her during the last five years. This person, though a villain of the first magnitude, had nevertheless, by long practice in the insidious arts of seduction, become an adept in dissimulation, so that he had actually secured the good opinion of every person of condition in and about Oxfordshire—consequently, was received into all parties of pleasure with a hearty welcome; and was never parted with but with regret. He was remarkably assiduous in congratulating myself and wife on our late union, and at length received an invitation to pay us a visit in London.

" One evening, as I was sitting with my wife, in one of the side-boxes of Drury-Lane theatre, Howard entered the same box, and seated himself over against us ; my wife knew him instantly, and welcomed him to London.   He seemed surprized at this meeting—I immediately recollected his features, and rose to salute him—he returned the salute in a very polite manner, and seating himself on our side, informed us in a whisper, that he had just arrived in town.   My wife and he began a whispering dialogue ; the subject of which was on her part, an enquiry about the people in Ox-fordshire.

" The play being ended, he very politely took leave, having previously received an invitation to pay us a visit the first opportunity, which he promised to observe.

" Some short time after, he paid the visit ; but as I happened to be abroad, I was deprived of the opportunity of seeing him ; which, I suppose, was no disappointment : For I have every reason to think my wife entertained him to his satisfaction.

" It is probable I never should have heard of this visit, had it not been for the following accident. Having received a letter from a gentleman of my acquaintance, in South-Audley street, which required an im-

mediate anſwer, I ſtepped into a coffee-houſe in St.
Jame's-ſtreet to write one, and juſt as I had it ſealed,
I obſerved a porter who had frequently carried letters
for me, paſs the window ; when I ordered the waiter
to call him in. When he came, I told him my buſineſs,
which he ſaid happened very luckily, as he then had a
letter for my lady, and as he muſt neceſſarily paſs
through South-Audley-ſtreet on his way to my houſe,
could very handily perform both errands at once.

"I was inſtantly tempted, by ſome unaccountable im-
pulſe, to open the letter which he had told me was for
my wife, and requeſted him to let me ſee the ſuperſcrip-
tion. He produced it ; and when I found it was a
man's hand writing, I felt ſo ſtrong an inclination to
peruſe the contents, that I communicated my wiſh to
the porter,—gave him a glaſs of wine, and promiſed
him a guinea. This had the deſired effect—he laid the
letter on the table, and told me he would call in a
quarter of an hour.

"I opened it carefully, and to my inexpreſſible horror and amazement, read as follows :

"CHARMING LOUISA,
" I received, and read with infinite pleaſure, your
" kind invitation, and ſhall not fail to attend at the
" ſtated period. We will then repeat thoſe ſweet em-
" braces which are to be experienced in your dear
" arms only. I have formed a plan, which appears
" to me more ſecure, as well as more convenient than

H

" the one we at firſt adopted ; which is to carry on
" our intrigue at the houſe of a friend of mine, in whom
" I can confide, where we may meet as often as eager
" defire can prompt, and enjoy the blifs of each other's
" company, without the leaſt danger of a difcovery.
" Send an anfwer by the bearer, and reft aſſured of the
" eternal love and attachment of   C. H."

" I waſ fo enraged at this indignity, that if either of
the objeſts of my revenge had been prefent, I ſhould
have facrificed them to my injured honor. I fuppreſſed
my rage, however, for that time, fcaled the infernal
epiftle, refolving to have ample vengeance. The porter returning, I gave him the guinea, and promifed him
five more; if he would let me fee the anfwer, to which
he readily agreed, and told me he would meet me at
the Horfe-Guards exaſtly at three o'clock. He departed and I knew not how to difpofe of myfelf until
his return ; for this difcovery had raifed my refentment
to fuch a pitch, that I was unfit for company or converfation. A hundred times I reproached myfelf for
breaking open the accurfed note ; then a fenfe of the
injury I had fuffered, awakened all my indignation,
and I was feveral times going home in order to pour
my vengeance on the head of my perfidious wife.
Tortured with fuch refleſtions, I wandered through the
Park—took a few turns acrofs the parade till the clock
ftruck three. The porter appeared in two minutes after.

" I retired into the paſſage leading to the treafury: He
followed and delivered his charge to me—then retiring

a few paces, left me to difcover the fulleft proof of my
wife's perfidy. The occafion and attention with which
I perufed it, made fo deep an impreffion on my mind,
that I think I can repeat it verbatim—'Twas thus :

   " MY DEAR CHARLES,

   " It affords me the higheft fatisfaction, to find that
" your love and attachment remain undiminifhed, and
" at the fame time, muft affure you, that mine are no
" lefs fo——Your hint of a new plan for the more fafe
" and convenient profecution of our amour, excites my
" curiofity to be acquainted with the particulars.   I
" am willing to affent to any propofal, that will en-
" fure us that uninterrupted, mutual blifs, which only
" fuch lovers as ourfelves know how to enjoy.   Don't
" fail to attend according to your promife ; for reft
" affured, I fhall impatiently expect the happy moment.
" May fortune prove propitious to our wifhes.
     " Adieu.   L O U I S A."

   " Conceive, Mercutio, if you can, the fituation of
my mind at that inftant. I never experienced fuch a
ftruggle between love and revenge before. I retired to
a tavern, where I fealed the letter, and returned it to
the porter. After enjoing him to the moft profound
fecrecy, I paid him the promifed reward, and he departed.

   " I fhould certainly have wreaked my vengeance on
the faithlefs wretch, but for the defire of punifhing her

co-partner in guilt, with my own hand. My mind was so violently agitated for some hours, that I found it impossible to form any resolution. After taking a serious retrospect of the matter, I determined to go home—behave as usual, if possible—mark critically every circumstance, and from the result form my determination.

"Having settled this in my mind, I walked about till dusk, by which time I had pretty well composed myself, and then returned to my faithless wife; who, Judas like, received me with a kiss. I was obliged to feign a flight indisposition, in order to avoid suspicion, as well as to procure an opportunity to stifle my indignation in silence.

"The next day I staid at home till after five in the evening, and perceived as the evening approached, she grew very uneasy—frequently asking me if I was indisposed. She also put me in mind of an assignation I had made, to meet some friends at White's that evening, and which I had absolutely forgot. When she mentioned this, I told her I would go. Accordingly I departed, apparently in a hurry. I walked down the street precipitately, and slipped into a tavern, posted myself at a window which commanded a full view of my house; so that nobody could have entered unperceived by me.

"I had not remained long, before I observed a man in a scarlet cloak, knock at my door: He was admit-

ted inſtantly; and though I could not be certain ̄whe-
ther it was the mark I was aiming at or not, it being
then duſk; yet determined I was to know who he was,
and his buſineſs there.

"Juſt as I got to my own door, I met one of my
ſervants coming out: I aſked him if any company had
come that evening. He ſeemed ſurprized, but replied,
he knew of none—adding, that Jenny (the chamber-
maid) had let ſomebody in a few minutes ago, and on
his aſking her who it was, ſaid it was her maſter. This
was enough: I made no delay, but going in, ſhut the
ſtreet door, locked it, and putting the key in my pocket,
proceeded cautiouſly up ſtairs.

"I liſtened a moment at the door, and heard enough
to convince me of my diſhonor. In a degree of rage
bordering on madneſs, I burſt open the door! They
were on the bed:—I drew inſtantly, and calling him
baſe villain—curſed traitor, with many other epithets
of the ſame kind, ordered him to riſe and defend himſelf; as I was determined to loſe my life or puniſh his
perfidy with death. He roſe with apparent reluctance,
and drew his ſword, which lay on the table, and put
himſelf in a poſture of defence. After a few paſſes, I
left him for dead on the floor—having run him quite
through the body. Turning to my faithleſs wife,
Madam, ſaid I, though you deſerve a ſimilar fate, yet I
forbear the ſacrifice: Perhaps you can find ſome ſub-
terfuge to vindicate your conduct to the world; but

confcience will not be impofed on. I therefore leave
you to the ftings of that monitor.

"Before I left the houfe, I ordered a fervant to go
for a furgeon, that if the wretch had any remains of
life, he might be faved if poffible. Whether he lived
or died I know not. I went immediately to my father's, and in as few words as the circumftances would
admit, informed him of the whole tranfaction. He
was much alarmed, told me I had acted extremely
wrong in committing fuch a rafh and defperate act :
However, as the thing was done, and as it was abfolutely neceffary for me to difappear fpeedily, for fome
time at leaft, he immediately wrote a letter to the admiral, with whom he was intimately acquainted, requefting him to appoint me to fome poft on board one
of his majefty's fhips ; at the fame time giving him
fome hint of the caufe of his making the requeft. He
then gave me one thoufand guineas, and bank notes to
four times that amount ; to which he fubjoined his
blefling, with tears, as did alfo my honored mother :
Both of them lamenting with me the fatal caufe of the
difagreeable feparation,

"I inftantly took horfe for Portfmouth, attended by
a fervant who is now on board. The admiral received
me in a very polite and friendly manner ; and when he
had read the letter, told me, he was very forry it was
not in his power to fupply me with any thing higher
than a firft lieutenancy, of a fifty gun fhip, having no-

thing better in his gift ; but affured me of the firft va-
cancy. He then prefented me with the commiffien
immediately ; and now, faid he, I will give you the
orders for failing, as that fleet muft fail with the firft fair
wind. The fecretary copied the orders, and the admiral, after fealing, delivered them to me, together with
a letter from the captain.

" 'The wind being fair when I came on board, the
captain, on reading the admiral's letter, hoifted the
fignal for failing. What has taken place fince, you
know already. And now, you muft confefs, that I
have had no fmall fhare of misfortune—neverthelefs, I
endeavour to eradicate the impreffions it has made in
my mind ; 'tis true, the refleclion gave me much uneafinefs for two or three days, but I find myfelf quite eafy
and cheerful now."

Our hero readily perceived, that the misfortunes
which he had experienced, were by no means equal to
thofe of his friend. He highly commended Charles's
refolution of leaving his wife to the fevere lafhes of her
own confcience, which, he obferved, would probably
be productive of better effects, than any corporal punifhment that could have been defired.

Nothing remarkable happened in the courfe of the
voyage. They arrived at Quebec in May 17. After
landing their troops, marines, provifions, &c. Sir
Guy Carlton gave orders for the fhips to be cleared,

and repaired, if neceffary, and to fail into a certain degree, and their cruize in order to intercept the French fleet. They were ready to fail in fixteen days. Their force confifted of two fifty gun fhips, and three frigates, all well manned and fit for either offence or defence.

The captain of the Manheim, of fifty guns, dying at Quebec, Charles was appointed to the command; in confequence, our hero left the Ifis, and accompanied his friend.

The period was approaching, in which our two friends were to be once more feparated:—The thick and gloomy clouds of adverfity were already collected, fufpended over, and ready to burft on the Britifh nation. Fortune had lavifhed her favors profufely on the king of England; but the meafure of his iniquity, being full to the brim, the goddefs took offence at the arbitrary proceedings of the imperious monarch, in conjunction with Bute, North, Sandwich, and feveral others of the fame ftamp, and was determined to humble their arrogance, by taking into her protection the oppreffed, much injured Americans, whofe deftruction was meditated, and every meafure that appeared likely to effect it, adopted in London, for no other reafon than that they would not tamely fubmit to be plundered of the fruits of their virtuous labour.

This favorable turn of affairs reanimated the fainting Americans, who laboured under every difadvantage but want of bread, courage, and a good General.

In England it had a different effect. The King and his fycophantic train were utterly confounded; for they had never dreamt of refiftance in America. They expected implicit obedience to their commands and demands, however tyrannical or unjuft. But the fequel demonftrated their miftake; and had fo remarkable an effect on George, that he became infane, and it is doubtful whether he is yet rational or not.

This fleet had not cruized long before they difcovered five French and two Spanifh fhips of war, bearing down with crowded canvas: The two latter were in the fervice of France. A council of war was immediately called on board the Ifis, wherein it was determined to attack the French (they were all under French colours) as foon as ever they came within gun-fhot. Accordingly, the neceffary difpofitions being made, the two large fhips bore up in front, in order to fuftain the firft fhock of the enemy's fire. The frigates at the fame time dropt aftern, with orders to act as opportunity or neceffity might require. Every man ftood at his ftation, with his eye fixed attentively on the approaching enemy—not a whifper could be heard on board. The fleets advanced to the conflict, with filent rapid motion. What an awful fituation! where thoufands of human beings ftand on the very verge of eternity! ftand ready to difcharge the dreadful meffengers of death among their fellow-creatures! Surrounded by the devouring ocean: Dreadful abyfs! fhocking idea!

The French commander call'd to the captain of the Isis to strike, otherwise to expect no quarter. He answered, that he wished for no quarter, and that if he intended to capture the English fleet, he must kill him first, for he was determined never to surrender while he had a living man on board. He had no sooner pronounced these words, than he gave orders to pour in a broadside, which was performed with alacrity, and returned no less vigorously. The fight soon became general. Chain, grape and langridge, flew like hail. Masts, yards, sails and shattered rigging, covered the foaming surface of the ocean, which, from the most beauteous green, was converted to a crimson hue.

The British tars, it must be acknowledged, fought with unparelleled bravery. Pity it had not been in a better cause. One of the English frigates taking advantage of the smoke to leeward, ran under the stern of a French ship of ninety guns, poured in a heavy broadside, which raked her fore and aft, and set her on fire, which was never extinguished till she was burnt down to the water. The frigate wore as she discharged the broadside, and recovered her position without injury or difficulty.

Just at that instant, a two and forty pounder penetrated the Blenheim, between wind and water, and was on the point of sinking before the leak was discovered—all hands were employed in repelling the common enemy, and therefore paid no attention to any thing elfe. At the fame inftant, the brave commander of the Ifis was deprived of his head and right hand by a chain-fhot. Before there could be any ftop put to the leak, the Blenheim funk, having three hundred and fifty men on board. Mercutio and Charles were on the quarter-deck when it went down : The principle of felf-prefervation prompted the former to feize a large hen-coop, which had worked loofe, by fome means, fo that when the fhip funk, it bore him up.

After having been toffed about for fome time, in the midft of this dire conflict, he, with nine of his fhip-mates, was taken into a boat belonging to one of the Spanifh fhips, immediately conveyed on board and hand-cuffed two and two.

They had fcarcely got on board, when one of the French fhips blew up—and while a fecond fhared a fimilar fate with the Blenheim, the fierceft flames de-voured the fails, rigging, and hull of a third. The explofion was dreadful; and a more horrid fcene was never defcribed. Legs, arms, heads, whole bodies, blood and brains, were hurled in the air, in awful con-fufion. The diftracted French failors were feen jump-ing into the fea, to efcape the more excruciating tor-ments of being confumed by fire. The flames having communicated to another of the French fhips, which encreafed the horror of the fcene. The two furviving fhips took to precipitate flight. The Englifh made a feint of purfuit, but being in a fhattered condition, gave

a great fhout, accompanied with three times three
cheers, hove about and let them go.   On their return,
they took up feveral of the miferable wretches that
had efcaped the flames, and fome few who had efcaped from finking with the Blenheim.

The French commander fteered away for Breff, and
preffed the Spaniard to accompany him ; but he abfolutely refufed—fo bore away for Bilboa, a rich feaport
in Spain.   On their arrival, Mercutio, with his fellow-
prifoners, were confined in a noifome dungeon, without light or frefh air ; the damp ground for their common bed, and a very fcanty allowance of courfe bread
and water, for their fubfiflence.   In this deplorable
fituation, they remained for the fpace of three months,
in which time fix of the unhappy captives expired; for
the horrid ftench of their own ordure, which was never
removed during their confinement, added to their want
of food and frefh air, introduced a malignant difeafe
among them, under which, thofe attacked by it, lin-
gered in extreme torture, about three days, and then
expired.   The wretched furvivors, envied their departing fellow-fufferers; and earneftly invoked the
powers of heaven to haften their diffolution—their
bodies were fo emaciated by the combined force of
grief, want and difeafe, that they refembled fkeletons
more than living men. Mercutio, however, in fpite of all
thefe, fuffered nothing more than want of liberty and
food ; for his appetite ftill remained, and although reduced almoft to nothing, was ftill healthy.

It happened, fortunately for our hero, that a Spaniſh nobleman having heard of the priſoners, made application to the chief magiſtrate for leave to ſend them to his villa, in order to aſſiſt at digging a canal, which was already begun, through an extenſive park, where a number of labourers where then at work.

The nobleman obtained his requeſt, on certain conditions, and diſpatched a domeſtic with the magiſtrate's order to releaſe them. When they were brought out, and their chains taken off, they concluded, they were going to be put to death. True it is, death never received a more hearty welcome, than theſe men would have given him. However, this was not the caſe, they were conducted immediately to the villa, whither the nobleman had already gone. When he was apprized of their arrival, he ordered them to be brought before him.

He was aſtoniſhed at their appearance, and expreſſed much indignation at the treatment they had received, generouſly commiſerated their misfortunes, and immediately commanded plenty of good food to be given them, after forcing them to drink a large glaſs of wine, each in his preſence. His orders were punctually obeyed, and two of the poor creatures inſtantly fell victims to the gratification of their raging appetites : They expired in ſtrong convulſions, while Mercutio and the other wretched ſurvivor, remained inſenſible for ſeveral hours. The nobleman, however, whoſe name was Don Diego de Guzman, ſent for a phyſician,

who, in a few days, by the application of salutary medicine, and nourishing, though simple food, restored
them to perfect health. After being shaved, washed, and
putting on clean linen, they began to wear the aspects
of men again ; but were still weak.

They were sent in company with several other la-
borers to digging the canal ; here, though they eat their
food by the sweat of their brow, yet, having plenty that
was good, with a quart of wine each man per day, they
recovered strength surprizingly, and began to experience much satisfaction. Mercutio, had he not been
greatly affected with the idea of the death of Charles,
would probably have been tolerably happy ; for having
experienced so many turns of fortune, he had become
in some measure, habituated to crosses and disappointment, and therefore, though his situation, at that time,
was by no means a desirable one ; yet it effectually secured him from the attacks of envy, and from falling
into those excesses to which young men are exposed ;
the effects of which, are galling remorse, tormenting
reflections, and very frequently, infamy. He therefore,
in gratitude, returned thanks to the Supreme Dis-
poser of every event, for the measure of contentment
he still possessed, in the enjoyment of sound and uninterrupted health and increasing vigour.

Don Diego generally devoted seven or eight hours of
each day in viewing the work and in giving directions :
Though a native of old Spain, and immensely rich,
yet he was neither indolent nor imperious ; but com-

pletely affable and generous ; in a word, fympathy and
benevolence characterized that noble Spaniard. He
had ftudied the features, air, and behaviour of Mercutio for fome time, with the moft acute attention, and
rightly judging he was of no vulgar extraction, refolved to queftion him on the fubject. Accordingly,
one day he ordered Mercutio to follow him, with his
mattock, as if to do fomething that had been neglected.   Having taking him out of the fight of his fellow
labourers, he made him a number of queftions ; fuch
as, where he was born? how he came to be captured ?
&c. The anfwer he received proved fo fatisfactory
to the Don, that he began to entertain a very high opinion of our hero's merit, and, after a paufe of fome
minutes,he afked him,if his liberty could be procured,
whether he would be willing to ftay and fettle in Spain ?
Mercutio did not refufe ; his anfwer however, was
evafive. He well knew that, being at liberty, a defire of
returning to his native country would inevitably predo-
minate.   He therefore framed his anfwer accordingly,
and, from the fucceeding circumftances, we may juftly infer that the old Don took for granted that he intended to ftay.

Don Diego told him to go to his work, and left
him. After the labours of the day were ended, a female domeftic came to Mercutio and defired him to
follow her. He complied, and fhe conducted him into an apartment he had never feen before ; and, after defiring him to fit, retired. He had not been long,

there before Don Diego made his appearance; and preventing our hero from rising, fat down by him.

Mercutio, faid he, ever fince I firft beheld you, I have entertained a prepoffeffion in your favour: I find that prepoffeffion has not been unjuftly founded. Your behaviour in the inferior ftation to which you have unfortunately been reduced, with the candid account you have given me of your misfortunes, confirms me in the good opinion I had conceived of you; and all thefe circumftances have concurred to determine me to fet you at liberty. To convince you of the fincerity of my profeffions, (here he rang a bell and a fervant entered bearing a bundle, which he delivered to his mafter and departed) take this, faid he, and with it your liberty, prefenting the bundle; which contained a rich Spanifh habit, embroidered; and though I propofed in our converfation to day, your ftaying in Spain, I did not intend to make that the condition of your liberty; as that would be only enlarging the place of your confinement. No, I have procured your liberty, and intend you fhall enjoy it in its moft extenfive latitude. You are at liberty to go when and where you pleafe. If you choofe to remain fome time in Spain, my houfe and my purfe are at your fervice.

Such a fuperior difplay of generofity in an utter ftranger, almoft petrified our hero with aftonifhment: He remained filent for fome time. At length he exclaimed, thanks to Heaven ! Thanks to the generous, the benevolent Guzman ! May that power who inspired you with these exalted sentiments, shower down his choicest blessings on you, and your posterity. May his mercy be liberally extended to you and them, as you have extended yours to me, exceeding my most sanguine wishes ! Command my life ! It's at your service—there is no injunction, consistent with religion and honour, you are capable of laying on me, that I can, or will, refuse to my generous deliverer—here he was interrupted by the Don. Mercutio, said he, I am already more than recompenced in the real pleasure I derived from a consciousness of having, in this instance, performed my duty. It argues a sordid, contracted mind, such as I hope the natives of Spain are strangers to, to confer a favour in hopes of retaliation : So I desire whatever thanks the effusions of your gratitude may inspire, may be directed to that Fountain of benevolence, who has commanded us to love one another, and who graciously inforced the precept by his own glorious example.—You will sup with me to night, and if you would oblige me, divest yourself of all restraint ; treating me in all respects as if we were sons of the same father. To-morrow I will give you a more convincing proof of my esteem : Which is greater, perhaps, than you expect. Thus this disinterested Spaniard suppressed the ardent acknowledgments which our hero was about to make, and which all mankind would allow him as justly his due : Desiring nothing but an approving conscience,

and wishing to ascribe all the merit of the action to the
Author of all good.—He then introduced our hero to
Donna Belvidera, his wife, a person of consummate
beauty and good sense, by whom he was treated with
all imaginable respect. The Don had two daughters,
who were accounted beauties, but they never appeared before Mercutio unveiled. After one month's residence there, no opportunity offering of procuring a
passage to England, he resolved to take the advantage
of the Don's proffer, and, having an inclination to go
to Barcelona the capital of Catalonia, noted for its
trade, riches and beauty, informed him of his intention. He instantly acquiesced, and, taking him into his closet, unlocked his bureau and taking out a
a purse containing 200 johannes, presented them to
him, saying, I insist on your acceptance of this trifle,
as a farther token of my esteem for you : It may perhaps be serviceable to you in your tour, in which I
heartily wish you genuine satisfaction : Barcelona is
a beautiful city, and one of the richest in the Spanish
dominions. I shall expect to hear from you in the
course of two months, for you may rest assured I am
much interested in your welfare ; and shall take a
pleasure in hearing of your health and prosperity.

Our hero was about to make a proper acknowledgment for this and every other favor he had received at
his hands, but was prevented by the Don's begging to
be excused for that time, as he was obliged to meet
some gentlemen on an important occasion. This put

an end to to the conference, and Mercutio began to prepare for his intended journey. Having procured a good horse, and being properly equipped, he took leave of the old Don and his lady, who did not part without regret, and set forward attended by a hired servant, mounted on a mule, a beast more frequently made use of there than a horse.

He made no delay, but kept steadily forward until he arrived at Barcelona, where he lodged some days at an inn, until he could procure accommodation in a private house, which best suited his disposition. He went one day into a jeweller's shop, to look at some trinkets, as well as to enquire for a convenient lodging ; and after some discourse with the jeweller, who was a very jocular person, and spoke tolerable English, received an invitation to dine. He accepted the invitation, and was conducted to an elegant back apartment, where his wife and four fine children were sitting. When the lady was informed that our hero was from London, she rose and gave him a very cordial reception, as she was a native of that city herself. Their conversation became general till dinner was served up. They informed Mercutio, that they were married in London, and had lived and carried on business near three years ; but the father of the jeweller dying, he was obliged to return to Barcelona, to settle his affairs and take possession of the estate. The jeweller further informed him, that he resided four years in London prior to his marriage, in which time he had embraced the Protestant

faith, and added, that he was determined to return to
that city, as foon as the war with America was at an
end ; as he found it very difficult to difguife his religious fentiments, though he ufed the utmoft precaution
for that purpofe—which line of conduct he conjured
our hero to purfue as he valued his life.

He fpent the evening with his new acquired friends,
much to his fatisfaction ; and as they had a couple of
rooms unoccupied, Mercutio hired them for himfelf
and fervant. He took leave late in the evening, and
the next morning, difcharged his reckoning at the inn,
and after providing for the accommodation of his cattle,
removed to his new lodging.

Here he began again to tafte the fweets of fociety ;
his hoft and hoftefs being perfectly frank, focial and
generous, which rendered his fituation very comfortable—his kind country-woman propofed a feparate table
for him ; but he requefted as a favor, to be permitted
to eat and drink with her and her hufband. This
was agreed on, and they enjoyed much fatisfaction in
the fociety of each other. During his refidence at this
place, he vifited every place of polite entertainment and
refort in that beautiful and opulent city, by which
means he contracted an acquaintance with feveral
young Spaniards of diftinction ; fome of whom pro-
feffed a very great friendfhip for him ; but among all
thofe, none had fo great a fhare of the efteem of our
hero, as Don Alonzo, a young Caftilian nobleman,

who inherited the moſt happy diſpoſition : To a very regular ſet of features, and genteel ſhape, he added an agreeable and graceful deportment—his judgment was ſound, and his converſation animating, modeſt and pleaſing. He had juſt arrived at Barcelona, after a reſidence of two whole years in the capital of France, that mart of vivacity and politeneſs, ſo that he retained none of that imperious ſtiffneſs of a Spaniard—neither had he acquired the extreme volatility which characterizes the French ; but that happy medium, which rendered his company very deſirable.

Alonzo profeſſed every ſentiment of reſpect for our hero, who fell nothing ſhort, ſo that in a little time a reciprocal attachment took place between them, which rendered their walks, recreations, and intereſts of every kind inſeparable.

Alonzo had a very extenſive acquaintance, to whom at different times, he introduced Mercutio as a reſpected friend ; by which means, he became, as it were, naturalized ;—and as he ſpoke the Spaniſh language fluently, his company was courted by all the moſt noble Spaniards in Barcelona.

Our hero with his friend Alonzo, and ſeveral other perſons of diſtinction, made an appointment to divert themſelves in chaſing the wild-boar, a kind of exerciſe common in that country. The company met according to appointment, and ſet forward in high ſpirits to

the chace. The dogs beat the low grounds for fome
time, and at length roufed an amazing large boar.

The foaming beaft took to an adjacent mountain,
and afcended it fwiftly. They purfued him vigoroufly
over the fame ; but on defcending the other fide, which
was very fteep and craggy, Mercutio's horfe was ftung
fo feverely by a tarantula, that he bounded fuddenly
over a fharp ridge of a rock, by which he difmounted
his rider, though an excellent horfeman. This unlucky
accident put an end to the fport, and threw the reft
of the company in the utmoft confternation. Every
one difmounted inftantly, and ran to his affiftance. On
examining, they found his right arm broke, and his
fhoulder diflocated. Alonzo mounted his horfe and
ran, or rather flew to a fmall village, which lay contiguous to the foot of the mountain, for a furgeon, who
dwelt there, and begging his attendance immediately,
went out and procured a horfe for him, in order to acce-
lerate his fpeed, which he had brought to the door juft
as the furgeon had his dreffings and implements ready,
—They foon arrived at the fpot where he was lying in
extreme pain. Alonzo immediately gave him a
large glafs of cordial, which greatly revived his
fpirits. The furgeon then got him removed to a
convenient place, and ordered a palanquin to be fent
for immediately, to convey him to the neareft houfe,
where accommodation could be procured, after the
opperation of fetting was performed. Mercutio's fervant was difpatched on this bufinefs inftantly, as there

was not one to be had nearer than Barcelona, which was full feven Englifh miles.

The furgeon, who was eminent in his profeffion, having examined, fet, and bound up his arm and fhoulder in an exceeding tender manner; told him he need not be under any apprehenfion, as he would pledge his life for the performance of the cure in the fpace of four weeks, with God's affiftance, if he followed his directions. The young gentleman, faid he, turning to the company, muft be carefully removed to fome houfe as near as poffible. A young Spaniard, one of the company, whofe father's feat lay but a fmall diftance from the mountain, propofed his being removed thither, where, he obferved, he fhould be carefully attended, until his cure fhould be effected. Mercutio, who by this time, was confiderably relieved from his pain, returned him thanks for his kindnefs; but afked the furgeon, if he might not be removed to Barcelona, without danger, and being anfwered in the negative, gratefully accepted the offer.

The fervant having exerted all his fpeed, foon returned, followed by a couple of brawny fellows, bearing a palanquin, in which Mercutio was immediately placed, in an eafy pofition, and conveyed to the gentleman's houfe. The fon having rode on before to inform his father, whofe name was Don Ferdinando de Caftigni, of the accident.

The old gentleman met the reſt of the company at the gate, gave them a cordial welcome, ſaid he was ſorry for the unfortuate interruption in their amuſement, and that nothing ſhould be deficient on his part to render the time of the young gentleman's ſtay in his houſe, as eaſy and agreeable as poſſible.

Mercutio was taken out of the palanquin and put to bed, and the ſurgeon having deſired him to be compoſed, till the morning, took his leave, as did alſo the reſt of the company, except Alonzo, who did not leave the houſe that night.

Our hero was bleſſed with a good night's reſt : His friend Alonzo had been twice at his bed-ſide in the morning before he awoke—the third time finding him awake, eagerly enquired how he had reſted. He anſwered, that he had never reſted better in his life ; adding that he had not felt the leaſt pain, ſince he had laid down.

The ſurgeon appearing ſoon after, dreſſed his ſhoulder, but did not open the bandage of his arm, ſaying he would let it remain till the evening of the enſuing day ; and aſſured him, if he kept himſelf ſtill, he was not afraid but he ſhould be able to perfect the cure in fifteen days.

Alonzo ſat with him the greateſt part of that day : In the afternoon he took leave, with a promiſe to ſee

him early next morning. Mercutio parted with him
reluctantly, as he was not intimately acquainted with
young de Castigni. However, he did not want for
company in Alonzo's absence; for the old Don and his
son, sat with him, until they conceived it time for him
to repose.

Not a day passed that he had not two or three of his
friends to visit him. In short he was as well attended,
during the three weeks that he was under the surgeon's
hands, as he could possibly have been in England.
His arm was restored to its proper shape and vigour,
for which he liberally rewarded his surgeon.

As soon as he was able to leave his chamber, he
made an apology to the old Don and his lady, for the
trouble his unlucky fall had made in their house, and
at the same time returning his most unfeigned thanks
for the generous and polite attention he had received
during the time he had resided with them. Don de
Castigini prevented him from proceeding any further,
by saying, " Come, come, Sir, I request you will say
no more on this subject—humanity is a duty incumbent
on every person who professes christianity; to have
done less, for a person in the situation you were when
first introduced here, would have disclosed a very callous
heart, an unchristian-like disposition, that would dis-
grace a Heathen, and consequently beneath a Christian.
But, however, as I see you are desirous of making a
suitable return for the little service you have received

K

in my houfe, I will foon give you an opportunity of
difplaying your gratitude to advantage." Make your
own conditions, replied Mercutio, and you fhall fee
with what willingnefs, I will hazard my life, if required, in the fervice of my generous and kind
benefactor. " Well then," rejoined the Don, " the
condition is this : That you will favor us with your
company fourteen days at leaft. This is all I afk, and
after your profeffions of gratitude, I expect you will
not refufe me the favor."

To this he very willingly agreed, and the Don introduced him to his three daughters, whom he had never before feen. They were all beautiful, and each of
them attired in a rich Spanifh undrefs, of blue fatin,
fpangled with filver. The two eldeft were a little in-
clined to brown, though beautifully featured ; but the
youngeft poffeffed all the beauty that could poffibly be
comprized in one woman. They dropt their veils when
Mercutio entered the apartment with their father ;
but he ordered them to unveil, and converfe without
referve, as though no ftranger was prefent. They o-
beyed, and the effect of fuch a fudden blaze of beauty, flafhing all at once on our hero, greatly embarraffed
him : However, he advanced to falute them, and
they met him with congratulations on his recovery.
He returned their compliments in a very modeft, becoming ftyle.

They had juft feated themfelves, when Alonzo and
young Ferdinando entered. After mutual falutations

and congratulations had paffed between them, they entered into an animated ftrain of converfation, wherein the young ladies bore a diftinguifhed part.   The
agreeable and pertinent remarks which, with the moft
engaging modefty they expreffed, afforded Mercutio
the moft fuperior fatisfaction.   Donna Ifabella, the
youngeft daughter, whofe perfonal charms were,
though matchlefs, totally eclipfed by the real and more
lafting beauties of her mind, made an impreffion on
the heart of our hero, not eafily defcribed.   To the
moft happy turn of wit, fhe united the fweeteft temper, and the moft critical propriety of fpeech: All
thefe amiable qualifications rendered her converfation
delighting.   'Twas this captivated Mercutio.   When
Ifabella took any part in the converfation, he was
in extacy ; with the moft profound attention he liftened to the enchanting accents fhe pronounced, and
when fhe ceafed to fpeak, preferved his attentive attitude, as if petrified with pleafure by the ravifhing
found.

A collation was ferved up, confifting of the luxu-
ries of Europe ; which was followed by a defert of the
choiceft viands of Spain, and the evening was fpent
in the moft undiffembled mirth and hilarity ; Don
Ferdinando himfelf being a very focial perfon, his
frank and affable behaviour confiderably augmented
the fatisfaction of the whole company.

The next day, our hero wrote to his friend and benefactor, Don Guzman, at Bilboa : His letter contained a moſt grateful acknowledgment of the obligations
he lay under to him—an account of the accident he
had met with, and his recovery, and concluded with a
promiſe to ſee him in a ſhort time, being determined
to ſet out for Bilboa in a few days.

Though Mercutio certainly intended to fulfil his promiſe in its fulleſt extent, yet he ſoon found (what he
might be ſuppoſed to have been well acquainted with
before) that nothing earthly is entitled to our confidence ; but that all our actions are guided by an in-
viſible power ; and that however flattering our future
proſpect may appear to our partial ſight, or however
near, yet the clouds of diſappointment and adverſity,
which are driven about by the uncertain gales of fortune, may intervene and deprive us of the glittering
phantom, if not forever, at leaſt for a ſeaſon.

It was with the utmoſt reluctance that Don Ferdinando and his family permitted our hero to depart, after a ſtay of twenty four days, nor then, without the
moſt preſſing invitations to pay them another viſit
ſhortly. A ſtrict regard to truth conſtrained him to inform them of his intention of leaving Spain very ſoon.
This information had a remarkable effect on the countenance of Donna Iſabella. Mercutio, however, in
compliance with the requeſt of the whole family, promiſed to pay them a parting viſit.

The countenance of Isabella resumed its wonted
serenity, and they took a cheerful and friendly leave
of each other ; he returned to Barcelona, accompanied
by Alonzo and young Ferdinando. His kind host and his
wife were happy in seeing him safe again, and, in tes-
timony of the pleasure they derived from his return,
devoted the day to mirth and good cheer: The only
thing that occurred to damp their joy, was the reflection of so soon parting with Mercutio: However,
they spent the day very agreeably. In the evening,
Alonzo and his friend took an affectionate leave of
our hero, and his host, and departed. Mercutio having retired to his apartment, began to reflect on the
long series of adventures he had run through since his
departure from his native country, which appeared
like a chasm in his life : The result was, he resolved to
stay about one week longer in Barcelona, take leave
of his friends there, and return to Bilboa, where he
intended to take shipping for England. But alas, how
vain are the resolutions of man ! When the idea of
taking leave of Castigni's family presented itself, the
image of the charming Isabella, arrayed in all the
charms peculiar to innocence, youth, and beauty, dif-
solving in tears at the separation, accompanied it.
However, as he supposed his heart was entirely disen-
gaged, he persisted in his resolution, and under this
impression endeavoured to compose himself to rest,
but in vain, the pleasing phantom was still visible to the
eye of his imagination ; all his reflections served but
to increase his perplexity ; nor could he sleep until Au-

rora had tinged the oriental clouds with ftreaks of the deepeft crimfon ; then the God of fleep gently advanced, and fpreading his downy pinions over him, lulled him into a pleafing flumber, where we will leave him to his repofe, and as Ifabella is foon to be introduced, as a principal character, we will en-quire how fhe fpent the night.

We find, from her own confeffion, that fhe paffed that night in no lefs perplexity than Mercutio. When. fhe anticipated the fatal, approaching day which was to feparate her from him for ever, her tender bofom fwelled with fighs; and fhe wet her pillow with her tears. Oh! fhe would exclaim, how unhappy am I! Though I enjoy all the advantages of birth, fortune, and education, yet my prophetic foul forbodes my future mifery. I love Mercutio, yet he is ignorant of it! What then ? Perhaps if he was convinced of the love I bear him, he would not have it in his power to extricate me from the wretchednefs which awaits me, or which would complete my mifery. Perhaps fome Englifh beauty is now impatiently waiting his return, to crown her happinefs by fulfilling the ten-der engagements he entered into, when they parted. And yet, my eyes deceived me, or I obferved fomething like embarraffment in his countenance to day, at parting. But what will that avail me ? It may be, if unen-gaged elfewhere, he has become enamoured with one of my fifters :—There ruin ftares me in the face again! Would to heaven I was acquainted with his fentiments; my heart tells me he is fincere; and, if I am not miftaken, would difclofe his fentiments on this fubject, if I could find means to propofe the queftion to him. But why fhould I wifh to know what perhaps would plunge me into the depths of defpair? Sleep at length overpowered her; but all her waking ideas paffed in review before her while fleeping, fo that fhe arofe without refreshment or determination. But to return :—

Mercutio arofe without that tranquillity of mind with which he had been bleft for a confiderable time before. He concealed his uneafinefs from his kind hoft and lady during the time they fat at breakfaft; and afterwards dreft, and walked out to one of thofe delightful gardens which are adorned with all the beauties of nature and of art, and are fitted for the entertainment and reception of perfons of quality only. He walked about; mufing on the vifion of the preceding night, for fome time. He reflected that the paffion which he had conceived was as yet but in embryo, and might be eafily eradicated. Befides he had no foundation to build his hope on, if he fhould cherifh it. When he confidered the difappointments and dangers he had already experienced, the loffes he had fuftained, and the depths of mifery to which he had been reduced, in confequence of his paft amours, he refolved to abandon an enterprize which appeared to be fraught with hazard and manifeft difficulty. He became cheerful again, and determined to leave Barcelona, in a very few days. At dinner he communicated his intention to his hoft, without the leaft hint of the reafon of fo precipitate a retreat. He difpatched his fervant, in the evening, to Don Ferdinando's, to inform the family that, if agreeable he would do himfelf the honour to pay them a vifit early in the fucceeding day. His meffage was received with pleafure by the whole family, efpecially by Ifabella.

In the morning he fet out, on horfe back, attended by a fervant. He was received with the fame degree of kindnefs, which he had uniformly experienced in that family. Though he was treated as ufual, yet he perceived that the apparent cheerfulnefs of the whole family was only the effect of his prefence : He perceived fome latent grief in their countenances, ftruggling to conceal itfelf from his obfervation : The day, however, was fpent very agreeably : A natural effect of the fociety of perfons of refined and generous fentiments. In the evening our hero informed them of his intention of fetting out for Bilboa in three days, at fartheft. This information had an inftantaneous and vifible effect on Ifabella ; (perhaps to Mercutio only :) fhe withdrew, but returned fhortly, more cheerful, apparently, than fhe had been that day. The moment of departure was procraftinated until a very late hour : At length, however, it arrived. Ifabella was the laft perfon of whom he took leave. To defcribe the agitation of his foul, in that moment, ex-

feels the power of my pen. His pulfe beat high, and he ftool as if riveted to the floor. The lovely Ifabella, whofe heart, tender as the orb of fight, had caught the fweet infection, was feized, when he took her hand, with a fudden tremor, which thrilled like lightning through the deepeft, and moft intricate recefles of it.—In vain fhe endeavoured to conceal the palpitation of her convulfed breaft—to withhold the fpeed of the glittering globes of chryftal which privately ftole down her blufhing cheeks,—Cupid had planted one of his keeneft darts in her unfullied breaft, and fhe tacitly confeffed it. Mercutio had addrefs enough to conceal his perturbation from all but her whofe fympathetic foul reverberated each figh, and felt each throb that agitated his difordered mind.—They parted.

Neither his ride home, or a retrofpect of his paft difficulties, could extinguifh or diminifh the flame which that beauteous female Spaniard had kindled in his breaft. I muft, faid he, I muft again fee Ifabella !—I behaved very ill at parting ! I muft difclofe my paffion to her ! —She feemed to pity my diftrefs in the parting moment ! Perhaps the little God has been propitious— has infpired her with ideas favourable to my wifh !— It muft be fo ! Her eyes betrayed the fecret of her heart, and feemed to fay, cruel Mercutio !—Can you then leave me ? Leave me thus ! O let me fee you once more ! Once more, e'er the relentlefs ocean for ever feparate us ! —Thus he wafted the night ; but, on being informed by his hoft that a veffel belong-

ing to Holland was to sail in the course of four or
five days he relinguished the notion of re-visiting
Isabella ; and resolved, if passage could be obtained
on board the Dutch vessel, to sail in her, and instead
of going to Bilboa, to send a letter to Guzman, to
inform him of his embarkation, and likewise that he
would make him complete satisfaction for all his kindness, on his arrival in England.

He sallied forth without making his intentions known
to his host, in order to go on board the Dutchman,
and, if he found things to his mind, to agree for his
passage ; but he had not walked fifty paces when a
billet was put into his hand by a female, who told him
she would meet him, in an hour, on that spot to receive his answer—she instantly disappeared. He was
surprized at the incident ; but did not open the billet
until he had returned to his lodging : Then locking
his door, he opened it, and read as follows.

"CHARMING STRANGER,

" If, on perusing those lines, you find I have ex-
" ceeded the limits prescribed to my sex, I pray you
" not to impute it to levity, or immodesty ; but to a
" passion which levels all distinction, and which
" constrains me to disclose to you a secret dear to my
" repose.—I love you ardently !——Let me know
" whether your affections are engaged or not. Defer your
" journey a few days—sincerity in your answer will
" be productive of a full explanation of my present situa

" ation, which is a very unhappy one —Your honour
" I depend on for fecrecy in this matter.—Your com-
" pliance will afford infinite pleafure to

      "ISABELLA DE CASTIGNI."

The moſt frightful fpectre that was ever defcribed,
entering his chamber at midnight, could not have
deranged his ideas more than this ſhort epiſtle did.
He faw all his plans difconcerted, and all his late
refolutions tumbled into the duſt in a moment.——
Though the epiſtle was not long, nor the requifition
unfair ; yet to form a proper anſwer to it, in fo ſhort
a time was an arduous taſk.—In the firſt place, he
rightly judged, if he ſhould give her encouragement,
ſhe would propofe an elopement ; this from principles
of honour he could not agree to, or if he could, it
would inevitably draw down the refentment of her
father and brother on his head. In the fecond, if he
ſhould renew his vifits at her father's, and ſhould even
procure his permiſſion to pay his addreſſes to her,
the known diḟerence of religious fentiments between
the natives of England and thofe of Spain would naturally produce a fcrutiny with refpect to his particular profeſſion, which might be attended with difagreeable confequences. However, time being ſhort,
he wrote the following anſwer.

      "LOVELY ISABELLA,
   " To be honored with your attention fo much as I
   " have this day, is a happinefs exceeding my moſt fan-

" guine expectations ; but your confidence in a mat-
" ter fo interefting as that of your love, is felicity
" too great.—You afk if my affections are unengaged ?.
" I anfwer no——yet——My affections were per-
" fectly fo, before I faw Don Ferdinando's fair
" daughter.—You fay your fituation is unhappy ! Let
" me fee your explanation fpeedily—Whatever is in
" my power to do (with honour) to render you hap-
" py, fhall be done, at the rifk of my life. Rely on
" my filence.   Adieu.

" M E R C U T I O."

This he fealed, and repairing to the appointed fpot,
delivered it to the female meffenger, who was already
waiting. He flipt into her hand, with a note, a fmall
prefent, and fhe inftantly departed.

At all events Mercutio was determined to make
enquiry about the Dutch veffel. Accordingly meeting a Dutch merchant at the water fide, he enquired
of him whether the veffel bound for Holland had failed
yet, or not ? The merchant informed him that fhe
had not : But that the captain expected to fail in lefs
than a week. He made no further enquiry at that
time, except the captain's name, and where he lodged :
Having received this information he repaired to his
lodgings.

The next day, fitting at a window fronting the ftreet,
he perceived the fame perfon who had brought him

the letter, pafs on the other fide of the ftreet : He inftantly followed her, and received the following letter
from her hands. As fhe had fome other bufinefs in
town, fhe told him fhe would return in two hours, in
which time he might have his anfwer prepared.

Having returned to his lodging, he opened the letter
and read :—

" ACCOMPLISHED MERCUTIO,

" Your affections, then, were unengaged before you
" faw De Caftigni's daughter——Oh ! might I be that
" happy daughter ! You are willing, too, to rifk your
" life to render me happy.—This is kind ; but if to
" eftablifh my happinefs requires fo precious a facri-
" fice, may I live in wretchednefs and die in obfcurity !
" —I fhall now give you my promifed explanation,
" and leave you to judge whether my fituation is un-
" happy or not.—Five years ago, an old Italian noble-
" man, of a vaft eftate, having rendered my father
" a very important fervice, by tranfacting fome
" bufinefs in Italy, at a critical juncture for him.
" Having fome bufinefs in Barcelona, he paid my
" father a vifit to inform him of, and congratulate
" him on, the fuccefs of his affairs. My father, na-
" turally generous, confequently grateful, received
" him in all the warmth of ecftafy, and thinking no
" reward too great for the fervice he had rendered him,
" bid him demand any thing he poffeffed.—He an-
" fwered, that he had no pecuniary views in conduct-
" ing the bufinefs ; but, as it was left to himfelf to

L

" point out a fuitable reward, he requefted his young-
" eft daughter in marriage. My father replied, my dear
" friend, your requeft cannot be granted : She is but
" juft turned of thirteen years, confequently unfit for
" marriage ; I have two other daughters, who are of
" riper years, if either of them has charms fufficient
" to engage your affections, I promife you my free
" confent to marry her, and I will give her a dowry
" fuitable to her birth and noble alliance.—He evad-
" ed this propofal by offering to remain unmarried
" four years longer, if my father would pledge his ho-
" nour to deliver me into his arms at the expiration
" of that term : The time is almoft at an end—Fifteen
" days will complete my mifery. The fupperannuat-
" ed wretch, who is near feventy, arrived here yefter-
" day evening with a pompous retinue. My father
" has never ceafed to lament his rafhnefs in making
" fuch an unlimited promife, and would give a third of
" his fortune to be releafed from the performance of it.
" —Oh Mercutio ! Do not fuffer me to be made
" wretched, forever wretched, but contrive fome means
" to fnatch me from the gulph of mifery, which, even
" now yawns to receive me ! Delay may prove dan-
" gerous—He is anxious for the confummation of his
" imaginary happinefs, and may, perhaps, find means
" to have the ceremony performed before the long
" appointed day arrives : If this fhould happen, death
" fhall deprive him of his long expected bride.—I
" have a maiden aunt in Barcelona, and have the con-
" fent of my father and mother to vifit her to-morrow
" —I will fee you to-morrow evening, at the place

" where you receive this, in order to put your genero-
" fity to the teft. If you are, as you fay, willing to ren-
" der me happy, you will fympathize in my diftrefs,
" and generoufly afford me your protection.—I am
" willing to go to the moft remote quarter of the globe
" with my dear Mercutio—No dangers, however
" great, fhall deter me—I will bid an eternal farewel
" to my native country, to the moft indulgent of pa-
" rents ; to the moft endearing brother and fifters, and
" to all the dazzling fplendor of wealth and grandeur,
" and, if heaven fo decrees, explore the earth's wide
" bounds, content and happy, if bleft with the compa-
" ny, and fweet converfation of my much loved Mer-
" cutio.   Fail not to meet me about dufk, mean while
" pity the diftrefs of the difconfolate

"ISABELLA DE CASTIGNI."

This letter awakened all his love for this unhappy
fair one. To fee her whom he loved with the moft fincere paffion, on the brink of being condemned to linger out her days in the arms of an old phlegmatic wretch,
for whom fhe had a mortal averfion. In forming a refolution how to act in confequence of the contingency,
he called to his aid reafon, gratitude, honor, and love.
With all thofe helps he was yet undetermined : He
figured to himfelf the impropriety of carrying off Don
Ferdinando's daughter, without his knowledge or confent ; and though love feemed to triumph over every
confideration, yet he could not by any means reconcile
himfelf to a breach of honour : Efpecially in fo deli-

cate a point. He refolved to meet Ifabella, however, according to her requeft—He did fo, and every fcruple was inftantly removed. She came attended by her faithful confidante—After the firft falutation, Mercutio propofed retiring to his lodgings. This was rejected, and Ifabella informed him that fhe commanded a private apartment in the houfe of her aunt, where they might difcourfe without interruption. He eagerly embraced the offer: The more fo, as it might convince her of the rectitude of his intentions. Thither, then, he was immediately conducted. The maid led them to an apartment in the back part of the houfe, and retired.

Ifabella then confirmed the contents of her laft letter, adding that her fufpicions of the Italian's contriving to haften the nuptials were not without foundation; for that he had abfolutely extorted a promife from her father, of fhortening the time by eight days. I have, faid fhe, obtained leave to fpend three days with my aunt; in which time, if Heaven fhall interpofe in my favor, by pointing out an efcape from this detefted wretch, my peace of mind will be reftored; if not—you know my refolution—I crave your affiftance—There does not exift a perfon fo capable of affording me the fame relief and protection with yourfelf: If this is withheld, I die miferable. Tears forbid further utterance. " Weep not, my angel," faid our hero, tenderly embracing her : " Thefe tears unman me ! Every thing poffible fhall be done; and even impossibilities attempted, to restore you to happiness." She brightened at this assurance, and he began to paint the obligations he lay under to her father, in the most striking colours. He then expatiated largely on the blackness of ingratitude; and concluded, by declaring the fervency of his love for her, which he said was heightened by the reflection of her being a daughter of the generous De Castigni; but added, that whatever steps a sense of her distress might prompt him to take in her behalf, he was determined to take none that should be dishonorable to himself; or by which he might forfeit the esteem of her noble father: " Such a step," continued he, " would render me unworthy of your confidence."

Our Hero expected the latter part of his declaration would have been a little unwelcome to Isabella; but in this he was mistaken: She told him she abhorred the very idea of purchasing happiness at the expence of his honor or integrity, adding, if she could have harboured the most distant thought of his being capable of acting in a manner unworthy of a gentleman, she should never have acted the part she had.

She then produced a letter from her brother, enclosing one from his mother. This letter promised a faithful attention to the request of his mother, which was couched in the following terms,

"DEAREST FERDINANDO,

" My foul is torn with anguish! Your sister Isabel-
" la's distress is extreme! Her misery is decreed!
" Her future life, if she survives the first shock, will
" exhibit nothing but woe!—Isabella loves Mercutio;
" Mercutio loves Isabella! They have declared them-
" selves: This day she has poured out her whole soul
" to me, and implored my assistance—your assistance!
" Five days more determines her fate!—What then?
" Meet her in Barcelona, at my sister's, on Wednes-
" day. My confessor, to whom I have imparted the
" secret, and who approves this step, will be there.
" Mercutio is honorable!—See their hands joined—
" the rest is fixed.—Remember this is a mother's re-
" quest, whose future happiness or misery hangs on
" this single event. What can be more meritorious
" than to render an affectionate mother, sister, and a
" sincere and honorable lover (who will by this means
" become a brother) happy at a stroke?——There is
" no alternative. Adieu.

" P. S. Come not here till sent for."

This letter determined our hero. Though a thousand different ideas crowded his imagination at first,
yet, when he compared all the circumstances; viewed the matter in every light in which it was capable of being viewed, he resolved no longer to refuse
a happiness, which, by the long concatenation of
events that had accompanied it, appeared to be

the immediate gift of Heaven: But to rifque every thing in eftablifhing that happinefs which involved his own. He embraced her with ardor, and exclaimed, "Is Heaven then propitious to my wifhes! And am I at laft to obtain that treafure, which is of greater eftimation than the glittering mines of Golconda! A treafure of which kings would boaft with rapture!"—Here fhe interrupted him by obferving, that her mother and the Reverend Father had maturely weighed every circumftance; that he conceived the Italian, having taken an undue advantage of a rafh vow, made in the effufions of gratitude, his claim had neither religion, reafon, nor juftice for its foundation, and confequently was null to all intents and purpofes; that if a countermine could be effected, it would not only be blamelefs, but meritorious: As the temporal, and, perhaps, eternal happinefs of Ifabella was deeply concerned, it behoved them to prevent, if poffible, a union fraught with fo many evils and inconveniencies. They alfo agreed that to deceive the Italian, without the knowledge or concurrence of the Don would be laudable, for the reafons above mentioned.

Our hero then enquired if fhe had feen her brother fince her arrival in town, fhe anfwered in the affirmative, and that he fhould fee him fhortly. She then rang a fmall bell, and Terefa, her maid, appeared: She told her to inform her aunt and brother that fhe wifhed the favor of their company. In a few minutes

they entered, accompanied by the holy Father, a perfon truly reverend in his appearance, the ferenity of
whofe countenance fpoke the goodnefs and tranquillity
of his foul.

After mutual falutations, Ifabella with her aunt retired into a clofet ; when the prieft began a very pious
and edifying difcourfe, in the courfe of which he made
feveral pertinent allufions to the caufe of their meeting.
He animadverted freely, and with great ingenuity on
the impropriety of hafty marriages, unequal matches,
rafh promifes, &c. and concluded by urging in a very
pathetic manner, the neceffity of the approaching union,
as the lives, and what was of infinitely more value, the
happinefs of the mother and daughter, wholly depended
on its confummation. . He next enjoined our hero to
write a letter to his intended father-in-law, containing
an ample account of the whole affair—promifing to take
charge of it himfelf, and deliver it to the Don, after
preparing him for the reception of the news. This
Mercutio promifed to do. They were then re-joined
by the old lady, leading forward Ifabella, the cheerfulnefs of whofe lovely countenance but faintly typified
the exquifite felicity of her foul, which heightened her
charms to a degree fcarcely inferior to abfolute perfection.

The ceremony was dignified by the fincere devotion
with which it was performed. The old lady, for the
firft time, performed the part of a mother, and young

Ferdinando that of a father, in conferring on Mercutio
a treafure which he would not have exchanged for the
empire of the univerfe.   The ceremony over, the prieft
and Ferdinando took leave under a promife of taking
breakfaft with the bride and her hufband the next
morning.

The hour for repofe arriving, the old lady conducted
her niece to a proper apartment, and retired, leaving
her under the conduct of her maid, as the bufinefs of a
bride-maid having never fell within her fphere.

The firft thing that occupied our hero's attention in
the morning, was a letter to his father-in-law, which
he penned agreeable to his promife, informing him of the
rife, progrefs and confummation of his prefent happinefs :
Explaining, in the moft refpectful terms, the motives
of his conduct, and humbly requefted him to pardon a
crime which originated merely from a wifh to reftore
to happinefs a family, for every branch of which he
entertained the higheft fentiments of gratitude and
efteem.   After finifhing this letter, he wrote another to
his old benefactor at Bilboa.

The prieft and Ferdinando kept their appointment,
and they all breakfafted together very cheerfully ; the
former, having taken charge of the letter, and wifh-
ing our hero and his bride a great deal of happinefs,
departed. Mercutio then informed his wife and friends
his wifh to embark for Holland as foon as poffible.

They were well pleased with the information, and Ferdinando promised to spend every evening with them, until their embarkation, and to see them safe on board. He then took leave and Mercutio went in search of the Dutch captain. He found him, and agreed immediately for their passage. The captain proposed sailing the next day, as he had to touch at Marseilles for some lading ; and observed, that if he thought proper to wait his return to Barcelona, he would lay too and take them in. This proposal, however, did not exactly tally with the circumstances of our hero ; he therefore, made a virtue of necessity, and told the captain he had some business at Marseilles himself, and was resolved to embark very early the next morning. They parted, and our hero immediately returned to inform Isabella of his determination. He next went to his lodgings, in order to satisfy his host, as well as to discharge his servant and dispose of his horse. As the servant intended to return to Bilboa, he committed the letter for Guzman to his care, which he promised to deliver safe ; and then presenting him the mule he had rode to Bilboa, the servant departed, very grateful for the liberal treatment he had received.

Our hero disposed of his horse to his landlord, and having taken a parting bottle together, he took a final leave of them, and returned to the impatient Isabella, who was afraid some unlucky accident would yet intervene to separate them ; she was, therefore, naturally anxious to leave Barcelona with all possible speed.

Ferdinando spent the evening with them ; indeed they did not go to rest that night at all—for as it might possibly be the last they were to spend together, and as they intended to embark with the first appearance of day, they were busy in making the necessary arrangements, and in concerting a plan for their future correspondence.

Before the day dawned, Mercutio and his brother-in-law walked down to the water side, as the former had appointed to meet the ship's boat at that hour. In the interim, Isabella waited on her aunt in her bed-chamber; who immediately arose at the sound of her opening the door, and taking her niece by the hand, led her to a cabinet, from which she took a casket, and presenting it to her, said: " Accept this, my dear Isabella, as a token of my love to you and my dear sister. May you be happy ! Perhaps I shall never see you more. Your father, when informed of the innocent deceit that has been practiced on him, will, I am convinced, search you out."

Just then the men returned, and the boat being waiting, they made ready instantly ; then taking an affectionate farewel, but not without tears on the part of the women, they set forward. Their baggage, was not very bulky, consisting chiefly of money and jewels, was easily carried to the water side by our hero and Ferdinando, who was resolved to see them safe on board. Preparations were making for weighing the anchor, when they came on board, where the captain welcomed them heartily, and conducted them to a very commodious cabin, which had been cleared out and fitted for their reception. The wind being favorable, the captain left them in order to get the ship under way as quick as poffible. The fails fet, and every thing put in order, he returned to the cabin, and informed Ferdinando that the ship's boat was ready to put him on shore, he took an affectionate leave of his fifter and her hufband, and returned to Barcelona.

Our voyagers were favored with a gentle breeze for some days, during which time they enjoyed as much happinefs as their fituation could poffibly afford. They happened to have a couple of French gentlemen and a very agreeable young lady of the fame nation, which greatly encreafed their fatisfaction. Social harmony, and convivial friendfhip were imparted from breaft to breaft, and uninterrupted tranquillity, a neceffary confequence of that friendfhip, feemed to be eftablifhed on a permanent bafis. But, as anguifh and rapture act alternately on the human mind, it is folly in the extreme, to dread the one or wifh for the other as permanent: For it is obfervable, that a continual round of what is generally underftood by the word pleafure, becomes by repetition, difagreeable, irkfome, and painful: Loathing and difguft takes place of defire—the tafte is vitiated, and the intoxication of the fenfes renders the agent incapable of diftinguifhing the difference between one and the other. Pain, flavery and chains, by long cuftom, become lefs irkfome, nay, in a certain degree, natural; and the anguifh of grief diminifhes in proportion to the length of its continuance.

Their tranquillity was not of long continuance, for when they were within two days fail of Marfeilles, they were overtaken by a dreadful hurricane, affifted by a ftrong current fitting out of the gulph of Lyons, which threatened the total deftruction of the fhip, and all on board. The wind blew with irrefiftable violence, which carried away the fore-top-maft and bowfprit in the beginning of the ftorm, and at length grew fo furious, that the main-maft went by the board, at the fame inftant the tiller-rope breaking, the man at the helm was knocked overboard; and it was at the manifeft hazard of their lives that the whole crew ventured to feize the tiller and bend new ropes to it.

Confternation and horror pervaded the minds as well as countenances of all on board, under a firm perfuafion of being fhortly buried in the capacious womb of the tremendous deep. Fortunately the fhip hull had fuffered no damage, for the mafts and yards which had been carried away, fell clear of the gunwale, and the rigging was immediately cut away. But as hope is generally the laft thing that forfakes us, fo they did not abfolutely defpair, till after enduring the fury of the ftorm for three days and as many nights, they found the fhip hulled, by the combined force of wind and waves, ftern foremoft into a cavity between two huge rocks, where fhe remained immoveably fixed.—

M

Despair at laſt ſtared them in the face!—Dreadful ſituation!—The ſhip's keel was jammed in between the rocks, from which no mortal ſtrength or ſkill could extricate it :—Surrounded by the foaming waves, which were hurled about in horrible confuſion, by the yet unabated fury of the tempeſt, they all betook themſelves to fervent prayer, and inſtant preparation for eternity! for death appeared inevitable.   Deſpair was ſtrongly depicted in the faces of the mariners, and every hope of ſetting foot on ſhore again had fled.

Five days and nights they remained in this horrid ſituation, and the major part of their proviſion, particularly bread, was rendered uſeleſs, the water being ſix feet deep in the hold ; however, they made very little uſe of what they had—they eat little, ſlept leſs, and in all reſpects conducted themſelves as perſons hourly expecting death.

Mercutio's concern for Iſabella triumphed over every other confideration ; his expectations of relief were exhauſted, he went ſeldom on deck, ſince aſſiſtance had become uſeleſs. The two Frenchmen, from ſimilar motives, remained conſtantly below, the one being the huſband and the other the brother of the French lady : They found it an arduous taſk to keep her in any tolerable degree of ſpirits ; but it muſt be confeſſed Iſabella ſupported her fate with a fortitude that would have reflected honor on philoſophy itſelf. About eleven o'clock, on the fifth night of their extreme diſtreſs, the wind ſhifted, and blew ſo violent, that the waves rolled

In fucceffion over this devoted fhip and crew. Their ears were at the fame time affailed with the moft fhocking peals of thunder, and terrifying flafhes of ethereal fire—floods of rain and refiftlefs gufts of wind roared in concert—the whole exhibited a fcene of terror which would baffle every attempt to defcribe.

As the ftern of the veffel lay confiderably higher than the head, the cabins and fteerage were yet clear of water ; the captain, his officers and paffengers occupied the former, and the common failors the latter. About day-break the ftorm began to abate, and by nine o'clock, they were bleft with a profpect of a calm fea and a clear fky. This, hopelefs as their fituation was, afforded them a tranfitory ceffation of grief, during which they all bent in gratitude to that Omnipotent Power, who had mercifully ftayed the fury of the wind, and awed the boifterous waves into fubjection.

Though this change in the weather had in fome meafure alleviated their diftrefs, yet the cutting reflection on their fituation, produced pangs of the moft excruciating woe : The beauteous profpect by which they were furrounded, ferved but to infpire them with the dreadful idea of foon terminating their days by famine. In this ftate of horrid anxiety, they fat as if benumbed and ftupid, until the captain broke the mournful filence in the following manner :

" My dear fellow-sufferers, we are in a dreadful situation I confess, but still we have the greatest reason imaginable to be thankful to the Almighty, for our preservation hitherto : And I look on our being cast on this rock as a most signal mercy, for had the ship continued to float, the storm was sufficient to have dashed her to atoms in a very short time, and which must inevitably have been her fate the instant she was thrown into this cavity, had she been in any other position. I sincerely believe that our being cast here was a means, employed by the Almighty, to convince us of our nothingness, and that he is not only able, but willing, to save to the utmost, those who rely on his Omnipotence for deliverance and protection : And although I must confess that appearances seem to contradict it, I really begin to conceive hopes that we shall all make the shore again with safety."

They listened with rapture to what he said, and eagerly demanded, what foundation he had to hope for what to them appeared to exceed the utmost stretch of human probability ? " Why, my friends," rejoined the captain, " the sea is now calm, and the sky clear, I will take an observation, by which means I shall be able to ascertain the best course to steer to make the nearest land."

The captain found by observation, that it would be most advisable to steer for Leghorn. " We are," said he, " thanks to the Almighty, all in good health

and vigor, we will get out the boats, and have them
fitted up with masts and sails ; the carpenter shall fix
the binicle in a convenient part of the long boat ;—let
every one take one hundred weight of his most valuable
property : With this burthen I am of opinion we can
make the port in three days, where I have a brother,
who can, perhaps, assist me in recovering a part of my
cargo."

This proposal was embraced with avidity by the
whole company, who immediately began to clear the
boats of all incumbrances, so that they soon had them
out and rigged, and then proceeded to embark the most
valuable of their effects, provisions, water, &c. The
captain, for fear of being separated by another squall,
proposed making a tow-line fast to the head of each
boat, by which, in case of extremity, they on board
the cutter would be enabled to get on board the long-
boat.

About four in the afternoon they left the wreck,
and steered away under an easy sail East by South.
Every one assisted, so that they went at a great rate,
using both sails and oars. The next day, land appearing on the larboard bow, they were inspired with new
life ; the captain assuring them they would be in Leghorn that night. Joy was imprinted in legible characters on all their countenances, and they congratulated
each other on the signal deliverance, as if they were
already on shore—they strove to banish the disagree-

M 2

ble recollection of their late diſtreſs, to make room for the more acceptable and pleaſing ſenſations which they already taſted by anticipation.

About ſun-ſet they deſcried a ſloop a head, at the diſtance of about a league, which they ſoon met. They hailed her, and requeſted the commander to come on board the long boat, which he immediately complied with.   This gentleman proved to be the captain's bro-ther before mentioned, who expreſſed much aſtoniſh-ment at ſeeing them coming from ſea in an open boat; but his ſurprize vaniſhed when informed of the particu-lars, and was much affected with the narrative ; but bid them be of good cheer, as they would quickly be among humane and hoſpitable people, who would render them all the ſervice in their power.

In about three hours they anchored before Leghorn. Being late at night, it was agreed to ſtay on board the ſloop till next morning, except the captain, who went on ſhore.

In the morning they diſembarked, and our hero hired one of the ſailors to carry his baggage.   He had juſt taken leave of his captain, and received his bro-ther's directions where to find ſuitable accommodations for ſome days, when, as he was handing Iſabella along, he was met by a gentleman in a rich Italian habit, who, after being informed of their ſhipwreck, kindly welcomed them on ſhore, and invited them to take breakfaft with him. They confented, and he conducted them to a very elegant houfe, where they were kindly received by the miftrefs. Among other enquiries, the gentleman afked Mercutio the place of his nativity? Finding him an Englifhman, which he was himfelf, he told him he intended to remove to England in a very fhort time, and politely offered him his houfe, if he would ftay with them : He added, that he expected to embark with his whole family in three weeks at fartheft.—Juft then a man entered the room, the unexpected fight of whom gave Mercutio no fmall pleafure : 'Twas George Wright !—The familiarity of the falutation of thofe two friends, amazed the whole family. But George foon removed their furprize by informing them of the very great intimacy which had fubfifted between them.

George embraced the firft opportunity of taking our hero afide, to enquire what brought him to Italy again. When Mercutio had fatisfied him in every particular, he in his turn informed him, that his wife had paid the debt of nature, fhortly after his departure for England. She fell a victim, faid he, to the fame difeafe which carried off my uncle and aunt. She was no fooner attacked by it than the moft unfavourable fymptoms appeared. On the eighth day the fever feemed to abate, which I interpreted as a good omen ; but in this I was miftaken, for that evening I obferved the phyficians bufy in private difcourfe, in the courfe of which, they frequently fhook their heads, as if void of hope. I.

suspected the truth.—The eldest of the three, both in years and practice, beckoned to me to follow him, and when in private, said: Endeavor, Sir, to collect all your fortitude, to support you under your affliction—To dissemble in such a case would be unpardonable—Your amiable spouse will soon be numbered with the dead! Six hours, without a miracle, will be the utmost period of her existence! I am sorry to inform you that her disease is of so complicated a nature, that it baffles the power of medicine. I have, with my colleagues, done every thing possible—we therefore, surrender her into the hands of that Being, with whom are the issues of life. He added no more, but turning about, left me in pangs of the most intolerable anguish.

His prediction was truly verified, for exactly at the time he mentioned, she expired in my arms! I must confess, it was the greatest shock I had ever experienced. I remained for some time insensible of any thing that passed; in which situation I was removed to another apartment, where, on recovering my senses, I found several of my friends at my bed-side, kindly endeavoring to alleviate my grief. Among the number who had collected to solace my melancholy, were two Franciscans, who entered into a very pious discourse on the subject of resignation, in which they did not forget to give me a modest reproof for neglecting to send for the Fathers of the Church, that they might have administered the sacrament (as they called it) of extreme unction, previous to her departure. A slight apology and a few

ducats, however, filenced them on that head ; but they
infifted on celebrating mafs on the fpot, which I did
not think proper to refufe.

The clouds of melancholy enveloped my mind
for a confiderable time, and it is doubtful whether I
fhould have refumed my native cheerfulnefs yet, had I
remained in Venice. I refifted the folicitations of my
friends a long time—at length, weary of their impor-
tunity, I refolved to purfue their advice, and, as I had
fome affairs to fettle in Naples, I made ready to go
thither immediately.

While I remained there, I went to Mount Vefuvius,
at leaft, as near as the ftones, fulphur, afhes and flames
would permit, as there was a moft violent eruption,
which covered the neighboring fields and gardens with
thofe combuftibles. From thence, I vifited the tomb
of the celebrated Virgil, which ftands at a fmall diftance from a fubterraneous paffage, cut quite through
the bafe of a large mountain, known there by the name
of Paufilipo's Grotto. I rode through this wonderful
paffage, and could juft, when on horfeback, touch the
arched roof, (which is perfectly regular, and beau-
tified with millions of curious ftones and fhells, neatly
arranged in every form that fancy can devife) with my
horfe-whip.

However, not to trouble you with a recital of every
place and thing I faw, in travelling from Naples to

Leghorn, I took my abode in this house, the owner of which is now my father-in-law, and as worthy a man as England ever produced. He then confirmed what the gentleman had told our hero, adding, that he was to accompany the family to England, and was highly pleased, when he found Mercutio was to be of the party.

Mercutio defired to be introduced to Mrs. Wright ; but George informed him that she was not in Leghorn, that he lived in St. Marino ; but told him he intended to set out next morning for that place, and requefted him and his lady to accompany him—declaring that nothing could give him so much pleasure and satisfaction. Our hero gladly accepted the invitation. They then joined the company, when George was introduced in form to Ifabella, who received his salute with the utmoft complaisance as her husband's friend.

The next morning early, they set forward, and met a cordial reception from Eliza, Mrs. Wright, who was as complete a female figure, perhaps, as Italy could afford. The modeft and fprightly behavior of this lady to her new acquaintances, unfolded a fweetnefs of temper, not frequently equalled, and never exceeded : In fhort, her whole deportment reflected the higheft honor on the choice and judgment of her husband.

The dwelling of George was fituated at the foot of a mountain, on the fummit of which ftands the capital

of St. Marino. A beautiful green of confiderable extent, lay in front of the houfe, terminating in an acute
angle at one end, and widening at the other in a gradual
manner, till it paffes the end of the mountain, and lofes
itfelf in a beautiful champaign country, diverf.fied with
fields, gardens, and delightful villas. At the back of
the houfe, at the diftance of a few perches, the mountain rofe with awful magnificence, in feveral parts of
which ftood fmall villages, and the interftices conf.fted
of rocks, caves and woods, affording the higheft gratification to a contemplative eye.

George, it feems, had fince his fecond marriage and
removal to St. Marino, taken frequent excurfions
through feveral parts of the mountain and villages adjacent.—In one of his morning rambles, he perceived
a path leading towards a high and craggy promontory,
which jutted over the fea. He could not fpare time to
examine where it led to then, returned home, and
thought no more about it, until one evening as they
were all fitting, enjoying the pleafant breeze, and admiring the diverfity of the objects which immediately
furrounded them. "Mercutio," faid he, "let us
take a walk: I ftumbled on a path not long before I
went to Leghorn, which, if I am not miftaken, leads to
fome romantic place, and I have a curiofity to fee it—
what fay you, will you accompany me?"—"With all
my heart," faid he, "come ladies, favor us with your
company." This was agreed to, and they all fet out
immediately.

After walking about a quarter of a mile along its base, they began to afcend the mountain by a narrow path, which led to a fmall village near the fummit. The path was too narrow to admit more than one at a time; fo George led them on, the two ladies kept the centre, and Mercutio clofed the rear.

When they had afcended to nearly the midway, George ftruck off into a fmaller path, which was the one he had mentioned. They had not travelled far on that courfe, till they came into a place which appeared to have been once cultivated: Here they found vines la'en with moft delicious grapes, of which they all eat heartily. George was not miftaken in his opinion of the place, for a more romantic fcene was never painted; but his having furveyed the promontory from the water, and obferving the direction of the path, enabled him to found his judgment truly. They all fat down on a flat ftone to difcourfe on the amazing fcene.

They were about midway between the bafe of the mountain, which in that part was wafhed by the fea, and the fummit. The fpot were they fat, projected over the foaming furge, which in vain attempted to wafh away its fupport, a huge pile of rocks, which rofe like a bracket:—Above their heads, from the fide of the mountain, arofe a ftupendous rock of marble, which likewife projected, in form of a femi-arch, making an awful, yet a magnificent canopy over the half of the old vine-yard. What particularly encreafed their aftonifhment, was the number of trees and fhrubs which proceeded in all directions from the fifures of that amazing rock ; for the contraft of colours occafioned by the various fpecies and pofitions of the trees, gave it the appearance of a fpacious arched ceiling, curioufly ornamented with tapeftry.

The ladies viewed this piece of natural architecture with the utmoft aftonifhment. With amazement, they caft upwards their wondering eyes, at the awful pile which hung over, and threatened to fall and crufh them to atoms. "Let us go down," faid Ifabella; "my eyes ach looking at this monftrous rock!" "The profpect is really terrifying," faid Eliza. As it was near fun-fet they agreed to return, and accordingly began to defcend in the fame order in which they had afcended. When they were near the foot, Mercutio, hearing a ruftling at fome diftance above him, turned about and perceived a man, ftep nimbly into the path which led to the old vineyard. He inftantly communicated the difcovery to the reft of the company, and they all continued to watch the Mountaineer, until intervening objects rendered it impoffible. They fet forward again, difcourfing as they went of the ftrange adventure of the man of the mountain. "That man," faid Ifabella, "is unacquainted with the nature of the place to which he is going, or is fonder of retirement than I am." "I am of opinion," faid Mercutio, "that he has fome fort of a habitation among thofe rocks. I will examine that place clofely to-morrow. I intended to have made fome farther ob-

N

fervations this evening, had not night overtook us, before we were aware. However, I will afcend to-morrow morning, before he is out of bed; will you bear me company, George?" "Yes, that I, will," faid he, "I am anxious to know who he is, and what he follows for a livelihood: "He muft have fome fingular reafon for taking up his abode in fuch a place."

At the dawn of day, George and Mercutio a-rofe, and, leaving their beauteous partners wrapt in calm flumbers beneath the calmy pinions of repofe, fet forward towards the mountain, in order, if poffible, to explore the rocky cavern, which contained the perfon they perceived afcending the preceding evening.

They arrived at the old vineyard juft as the fun-beams began to penetrate the horizontal mifts; and with the utmoft filence and caution, placed themfelves under a fpreading vine, fo advantageoufly, that it was impoffible for their game to efcape; nor was it poffible for any perfon to afcend or defcend by the path without difcovery. They had not remained in am-bufh long, when they perceived the broad ftone, on which they had fat the preceding day, rife, as if by magic art, and from the cave, to which it ferved for a door, iffued a young man richly dreffed, followed by the identical man they had feen the evening before, who reared the ftone againft the rock.

"Here William," (faid the young gentleman, in good Englifh) "convey this letter to my dear Teren-

tia ; do not return without an anfwer. Be fpeedy and
faithful ! If heaven favors my efcape from Italy, I
will generoufly reward your diligent and trufly fervi-
ces." The fervant vanifhed inflantly ; but our am-
bufcade lay flill, in order to make further difcoveries.

. The flranger, after walking backward and forward
in filence, with his arms folded, exclaimed aloud,
with all the marks of grief and anxiety in his countenance, " Why, O Why ! ye immortal powers, have
ye beftowed on me every thing that the world conceives
conducive to happinefs, and fuffer me neverthelefs,
to exift here a living monument of thy difpleafure,
fecluded from the fociety of mankind ?—If without
knowledge or intention, I have merited punifhment
extreme, O haflen my diffolution, by hurling the hif-
fing bolts of thy vengeance on my devoted head ;
and, at one ftroke, reduce me to a ftate of nonenti-
ty ! O that heaven had doomed me to a life of indigence ! Had doomed me to break the ftubborn glebe,
or to have furrowed the briny wave ! The peafant is
unacquainted with the care that hourly torments me ;
and the cheerful mariner performs the duties of his
ftation with alacrity and content ; but here am I, on
an eminence, the very idea of which is fufficient to
petrify a man with horror, unmoved at the dreadful
fituation, becaufe the extreme anguifh of my mind
is fuperior to the greateft corporal dangers."

This faid, he advanced to the identical fpot where the two friends were pofted, in order to indulge his melancholy under the branches of the cluftering vine. 'Tis impoffible to defcribe his aftonifhment, when he faw them both arife, and heard them falute him in Englifh ! He gazed wildly on them for a moment, then fpringing backward, ran towards the edge of the precipice, with a refolution to throw himfelf into the fea, and would certainly have effected it, had not Mercutio; who fufpected his intention, intercepted him in the midft of his career, and with the affiftance of George, took him by force, to the place where they had been fitting fo long.   Having feated themfelves, one on each fide of him, Mercutio in the moft foothing terms, attempted to fet his late rafhnefs in a proper point of view ; defiring him at the fame time, to fear nothing, as they were friends, and would give him all the affiftance in their power, and concluded by requefting him to compofe himfelf a little, to favor them with a brief fketch of his adventures, and inform them by what means he, got into that difmal retreat.

" Gentlemen," replied the aftonifhed youth, who could yet fcarcely believe his eyes and ears, " before I gratify your requeft, you muft anfwer me two or three queftions : Your appearance tells me you will do this candidly."   They affured him upon honor they would. " Firft then, were you ever in this place before this morning ?"   They immediately recounted to him the adventures of the preceding evening, not omitting

the moſt minute circumſtance. This information in-
ſpired him with freſh life : He then demanded if they
were natives of Fngland ? And being thoroughly ſatisfied in theſe particulars, he exclaimed in rapture,
Thanks to the immortal Jehovah! Deign to accept the
grateful thanks of an unworthy mortal, thou glorious
and inexhauſtible ſource of benevolence, for this interval
of happineſs in the midſt of my diſtreſs ! Pardon my
impatience—I am but mortal !

"Forgive me, gentlemen," ſaid he, "I behave very ill ; but I doubt not your generoſity will impute it
to the real cauſe." They requeſted him to make no
apology for his behavior as it needed none, aſſuring him
they approved his ſenſibility, and looked on it as
proof of a good heart.

Eugenio, the ſtranger, perceiving their impatience
to hear his ſtory, began thus :—" Well, gentlemen, I
ſuppoſe you have not met with ſuch a ſcene as this in
all your travels : If you pleaſe, we will deſcend into
my ſubterraneous habitation, which exhibits a lively
epitome of my own wretchedneſs." The deſcent was
very craggy, which ſupplied the want of ſtairs.   After
deſcending about twelve feet perpendicular, they found
themſelves in a kind of grotto; the floor of which was
compoſed of ſolid marble.   The roof was of a concave
form, lined with party-coloured ſhells, and ſtones of
different complexions and qualities.   The cave was
about thirty feet long, and fifteen in width: The end

next to the fea was entirely open, forming an arch ;
and that part which compofed the roof, projected full
fifteen feet beyond the mouth of the cavern, which
fcreened him effectually from rain. The profpect it
afforded was really terrifying : Nothing could be obferved at the back part of the cave ; but the terror was
greatly encreafed by cafting the eye downward from the
mouth to the dreadful cliffs which hung below. One
would be tempted, when viewing this fcene, to fuppofe that the author of the tragedy of Lear, was fitting in the mouth of this cave, when penning the
defcription which he puts into the mouth of Edgar,
in order to deter old Glofter from the defperate act of
cafting himfelf headlong from fuch a height.

In one corner of the cave lay a matrafs and
fome other bedding ; in another, a fmall trunk, which
ferved the double purpofe of table and cupboard : A
fmall kegg, and a brace of piftols made up the reft of
the furniture, all which had been procured and conveyed thither by the trufty fervant.

Being all feated on the matrafs, Eugenio proceeded
to relate his ftory :—" My narrative," faid he, "gentlemen, will be found barren of pleafure or amufement,
as it confifts entirely (the latter part at leaft) of
melancholy, vexation and defpair. My father, one of
the reprefentatives of the county of M——, thought
proper, after I had gone through all the fteps of a liberal education at home, that I fhould take a tour thro'

France, Spain, and Italy. In confequence of this refolution, he fought out an elderly gentleman, of
good morals, completely verfed in the fciences, a
competent judge of the human mind and the paffions
of it. He poffeft a fweetnefs of temper peculiar to
himfelf, and his countenance and deportment would
have commanded refpect among ruffians. Such a
perfon, inheriting every endearing qualification, could
not have failed to attract my moft profound reverence
and efteem : I already anticipated the profit, as well
as pleafure, I fhould derive from the company of a
gentleman, who knew how to blend the moft inftruc-
tive precepts with the moft familiar converfation,
from which I might imbibe principles that would reflect honor on the choice of my father, the abilities
of my tutor, and on my own genius and induftry.

" My father's next care, was to engage a faithful
fervant to attend us through the whole of our peregrination ; but fearing left a frefh hand, who was unacquainted with the family, might not anfwer the purpofe, he gave us his own valet, who ferved him in his
travels twenty years ago, and is the fame you faw here
to-day. I had juft entered my eighteenth year when
I commenced this tour. Our firft move was to Paris,
where we remained three months. From thence
we went to Orleans, ftayed three weeks ; and
then proceeded to Lyons. We made but a fhort ftay
there, refolving to embark at Toulon for Civitta Ve-
chia. We fpent fix weeks in Rome, and then vifited

Naples, ftaid there a fhort time and fet out for Florence,
which we never yet have reached. Having miffed our
proper road we travelled till we were within an incon-
fiderable diftance of the capital of St. Marino. My tutor, who had formerly been there, propofed, as we
were fo near, to ride into town, put up our horfes,
refrefh, and fpend an hour or two in the evening in
the governor's garden, which, he faid, was a perfect type of Eden—lodge in St. Marino that night,
and ftart for Florence in the morning. I made no
objection but fubmitted every thing to his fuperior judgment. The lanlord where we halted, fent a little Italian
with us to the porter of the governor's gardens, to requeft admiffion for us in his mafter's name. He informed the porter that we were a couple of foreign gentlemen on our travels, who had rode a confiderable diftance out of our way in order to take a view of the
gardens, and that his mafter would efteem the favor as
done to himfelf if he would admit us. He admitted us
without hefitation, for which my tutor rewarded him
with a piece of gold. He then conducted us to a walk
which led to the centre. I was ftruck with admira-
tion at the aftonifhing ftruggle between nature and art,
which appeared in the beauteous difpofition of the innumerable furrounding objects. In the centre, a bafon of
marble, well flocked with gold and filver fifh, fifteen
yards diameter, had a very fine effect, which was
encreafed by the figure of a fea-horfe, gilt, in the mid-
dle of the bafon, from the noftrils of which two ftreams
of water projected to the height of thirty feet. The

bafon is immediately furrounded by ten beautiful olive
trees, planted at equal diftances. Twenty yards from
thefe, another circle of trees afford a charming fhelter
to the delightful arbors which occupy the intermediate
fpaces. Here perfons of the firft rank in the republic,
ufually fpend their evenings, after feafting their fight
and fmell with the exquifite odours which proceed from
the flowers of every hue ; which, by the culti-
vating hands of the moft celerated florifts, are taught
to grow in every direction. In each of thefe arbors
is an elegant organ, which, by turning a fmall brafs
cock, plays off thirty-fix favorite Italian airs : They
can all be fet going together, or one, two, &c. at pleafure. The contrivance is a mafter piece of art : By
raifing a fmall gate in the fide of a canal at fome diftance, from which the bafon is fupplied, a fmall trunk
is immediately filled with water ; at the other extremity
of which are as many brafs cocks as there are organs :
When thefe are turned, the mufic begins. One of thofe
organs was playing juft as we paffed the door of the
arbor. We ftopped a while to liften to the enchanting
found, an Eunuch coming out at that moment, my tutor
enquired if a couple of foreigners might be admitted.
He defired us to wait a moment, left us, and inftantly
returning, defired us to walk in. We complied, and
were much furprized at being faluted, on our entrance,
by five ladies"—(Here he faultered)—" Five ladies
richly habited and clofely veiled." (Here tears interrupted his narrative. Recovering, " Gentlemen,
pardon my emotion," faid he, " you will find in the

sequel of my unhappy story, enough to justify my present behavior.

"We returned their salute in a proper manner. The music was suddenly stopt, and one of the ladies, who by her air and the superiority of her dress, appeared to claim the precedence, requested us to be seated, with which we complied. She then asked how long we had been in Italy? My tutor satisfied her in this particular, she proceeded to ask several other questions concerning our past travels, and the route we intended to take ; to all of which we answered without reserve. She expressed her satisfaction with the discription we had given her of England, France, and the other places through which we had passed ; and in her turn described in the most animating style, the innumerable rarities of Italy, adding, that three days would not be sufficient to review those gardens, as they were very extensive. We passed the highest encomiums on the taste, magnificence and convenience, which appeared in every part ; but urged the unavoidable necessity of departing from thence the next morning, as our time was limited, and we had spent a great portion of it in France ; therefore, it required our exertion, in order to finish our intended tour within the appointed time.

"To this she made no answer, but rung a small bell, which brought the Eunuch, to whom she whispered a few words : He withdrew immediately, but soon after returned, bearing two bottles, some glasses, and a casket of the most dilicious fruits. Having placed thefe on a table, he was ordered to fet the mufic to playing. The ladies invited us to partake of this refefhment. The mufic began, and the ladies unveiled.— But ah! The pangs that light has coft me are beyond defcription! The firft time my ravifhed eyes met thofe of the beauteous Terentia, my foul experienced emotions to which, till then, I had been a ftranger! Under thefe new impreffions I was much embarraffed, I retired for fome time, for feeling my face flufhed with an unufual warmth, I was afraid my tutor fhould perceive my agitation; weil knowing him to be a man of the moft acute penetration, and apt to draw the moft exact conclufions. I was convinced that the beauteous object who was the caufe of my emotion, perceived it plainly; for whenever my eyes accidentally met her's, I found them rivetted on me; fhe would then caft them downwards, and affect to be paying earneft attention to the mufic. Having walked once or twice round the bafon, I found myfelf pretty well compofed; I fummoned all my fortitude, and returned to my company. After the organ had played off a round, my tutor made a motion to retire; accordingly, having made a proper acknowledgement, for the very kind reception we had met with, we took leave and departed.

"We returned to our inn, and retired early to reft. When I reflected on our evening's adventure, I began to be well fatisfied at leaving St. Marino in the morning,

as the means of obliterating the memory of an infant
attachment, which, if fuffered to gather ftrength, muft
inevitably draw after it a train of difagreeable, if not
fatal confequences ; for by the influence the dear Terentia had over the reft of the ladies, I concluded, and
rightly too, that fhe muft be the governor's daughter.
My fleep, however, was much difturbed by dreams,
yet when my tutor awakened me, which was at day-
break, I found myfelf in tolerable fpirits. The reafon
he affigned for waking me fo early, was, that it would
be much more agreeable to ride in the morning, than in
the fcorching rays of noon. I rofe immediately,
and though the mandate appeared fomewhat difagreeable at firft, yet I dreffed brifkly : In the mean time, my
tutor roufed the landlord, and ordered our horfes to
be got ready immediately. My chagrin wore off infenfibly, and the vifions of the preceding night were entirely obliterated ; I became compofed and cheerful,
and began to anticipate the pleafure of viewing the rarities of Florence. My fervant was adjufting my hair,
when my tutor entered and informed us, that our
horfes were ftolen ! What then is to be done ? faid I.
Why, replied my tutor, we muft remain here a
day or two, in order that the landlord may have an opportunity of making a fearch for them, and if they are
not to be found, he muft pay for them, and we muft
endeavor to procure others. We had depofited a hundred guineas, the value of the horfes, in the hands of the
owner, but were to be reimburfed in Florence, by the
perfon to whom we were to deliver them, all but fifteen
guineas, which was for their hire.

" Being detained contrary to our wishes or expectations, my tutor, after breakfast, proposed taking a further view of the Governor's gardens, which pleased me
exceedingly. On our way to the gardens, my tutor
pointed to a superb edifice, which he informed me was
the palace of the Governor. We stood some minutes
to view this magnificent structure, and as we were
turning to go to the gardens, I perceived at one of the
upper windows, the lady who had treated us so kindly
the preceding evening ; but perceiving us, she instantly
disappeared.

" This incident gave me some uneasiness ; however,
I still supported a kind of feigned cheerfulness, in order
to deceive my tutor—the first time I had ever felt an
inclination so to do. Having gained admittance, we
took a different walk from that of the preceding day,
which led us into one of the most delightful scenes in
nature. Here, painting, botany, statuary, &c. were
carried to the most elevated pinnacle of perfection :
Endless beauty and variety attracted the sight, and the
most exquisite odours pervaded the whole parterre.
If there is a place on earth, descriptive of the primeval
residence of our first parents, this must be the spot.

" We traversed these paradisiacal walks until noon,
and the day beginning to grow warm, we retired into
an elegant summer-house, so situated as to screen us entirely from the meridional beams, and at the same time
to command a prospect of the circus, bason, &c.

O

" We fat difcourfing there for fome time ; my tutor, according to his ufual manner, philofophizing and moralizing on every perceptible object. At length, growing drowfy, he faid he would take a nap, and defired me to awaken him in an hour. After he had flept fome moments, I found myfelf weary fitting alone, I got up, and bent my fteps towards a fmall grove of trees, cut in the form of cones, and planted in narrow rows, which formed a very refrefhing retreat.

" I had not been long in this fequeftered fpot, when I faw four or five young ladies crofs the walk I was in, at the diftance of about a hundred yards. They turned their faces full on me as they croffed, but paffed along without hefitation. Though I was not fure they were the fame I had been in company with the evening before, yet I found an unufual flow of fpirits on their paffing, and was anxious to have a full view of them, for fomething whifpered me, There goes the caufe of your late uneafinefs. I immediately, I know not by what impulfe, advanced to the fpot where they had thwarted my fight. When I arrived there, I defcried them at a diftance taking leave of each other, after which each took a different route. I was convinced that I had gueffed rightly, for fhe whofe image had haunted me all the foregoing night, was then walking flowly before me, towards the farther end of the walk. Prompted by a motive too powerful for me to refift, I followed, without approving of my own conduct, and foon overtook her. Hearing fome body walking behind her, fhe looked round and I advancing, faluted her,

She returned my salute very ingenuously, and we joined conversation to the end of the walk, and entered an elegant rotunda, by which it terminated, where we discoursed familiarly on several matters, with the relation of which I shall not trouble you; let it suffice to say, that we not only exchanged vows of eternal fidelity, but formed an assignation to meet, that very evening, in order to enlist ourselves under the sacred bonds of hymen.

"I know, gentlemen, you will condemn my precipitancy; but if you reflect that love was the acting spring, my unhappy case will have a claim to your pity, at least. We parted, and I found my tutor still sleeping. I awakened him, and we returned, to the inn to dinner. In the afternoon the landlord returned, and informed us that he had got intelligence of the horses; but desired one of us to go with him, as he had taken very little notice of them, and consequently would not be able to prove them, if required. My tutor said he would go, and accordingly set out, and I have not seen him since.

" In the evening, I repaired to the spot where I was to meet the object of my love; 'twas at the entrance of a wood at the foot of this mountain. She appeared at the time appointed, and we at her request penetrated the wood about half a mile, to the mountain brow, where we were met by an old Friar, who conducted us to a cell, in the side of the rock, and, shutting the door, desired us to sit down. My

charming bride told him she was in hafte, and requefted him to perform the ceremony immediately, as he
had promifed.

"He then reprefented the imminent danger to which
he should expofe himfelf, and the magnitude of the
offence; adding, that he trembled at the fatal confequences that muft inevitably follow a difcovery. She
told him there was not a perfon on earth privy to it but
thofe who were prefent, and that as she intended to
fleep in her own apartment that night, there was not
the leaft shadow of danger. To thefe arguments she
added a purfe of gold, which effectually filenced the
reverend father, and fecured his fervice.

"He then proceeded to the nuptial ceremony, which
he performed in a very devout and becoming manner.
After the ceremony was ended, he laid the ftrictest in-
junctions on us never to difcover the place nor the perfon by whom we had been married. This we both
promifed religiously to obferve ; then, having thanked
him and wished him a good night, we were about to
leave the cell, when we were much alarmed at hearing
the found of human voices, approaching. Our confternation was increafed, when the Friar, who went
out on the firft alarm, came in and informed us, that
a party of the Governor's life guards, with an officer at
their head, were within two hundred yards, advancing
briskly, by torch-light. Imagination cannot shape
to itfelf a fituation more alarming than mine was at

that moment. The Friar said; "Fly my fon! Your being found here will be fatal to us all. I have a private way to efcape under ground; perhaps if you are not found, all may yet be well." There was no time for deliberation; I was conftrained to comply, Heaven knows with what reluctance! So, after taking a parting embrace, I fear for ever, of my dear Terentia, he gave me a burning, waxen taper in my hand; then lifting a trap door, beftowed on me his benediction, and I entered the difmal gulph, overwhelmed with all the horrors which fuch a dreadful viciffitude was capable of producing. He fhut down the door and left me to penetrate the bowels of this mountain for near a mile, under the moft excruciating torture of mind. At length, I emerged once more into open air, through a crevice of a rock barely wide enough to admit me. I wandered about through the thickets, fometimes miffing my fteps and falling many yards down the rugged fide of the mountain, till day light, when I found myfelf on the uppermoft declivity of this promontory, which affords a much more horrid profpect than you now behold. In that inhofpitable fpot I fat down, weary and faint with climbing from one ridge of rocks to another, all night, to bemoan my adverfe fate, ruminating on the dreadful fituation to which, in the fhort fpace of two days and two nights, I was reduced, the circumftances which produced, and thofe which accompanied this change; I became as it were, petrified with grief and aftonifhment, and remained infenfible of every thing, and fhould probably, never have recovered, had not my man, who providentially through curiosity watched us to the cell, and lay perdue till the guards were gone, discovered my retreat. He, observing that they took my dear spouse and the Friar with them, suspected I was slain, and as soon as they were out of sight, entered the cell.

" After he had called me several times by name, he began to search diligently, and finding a waxen taper, light it, and as he has since informed me, searched every part of the cell with great minuteness. He was exceedingly surprized, and could not believe his own eyes: Looking again, however, very narrowly, he espied the trap door, which he raised and descended instantly. He continued pursuing and calling me until his taper was exhausted, and then groped his way to the hole through which I had passed. It being then broad day, so that in some places he could trace my footsteps along. Observing something white, at a distance on an eminence, far above him, he advanced towards it, thinking I had laid down, and hung my handkerchief there as a signal to him in case he should search for me. However, in this he was mistaken ; for though it was my handkerchief, I was not there, but had dropped it by accident. But it happened through the providence of God, that as he stood debating with himself whether he should proceed, or return back by the way he came, and inform my tutor of what had happened, that he perceived me at the distance, he supposed, of three quarters of a mile, climbing over a ridge of rocks. He had once a mind to call ; but reflecting, that as I was ignorant of his having followed me, I might conceive it to be some of the guards in pursuit, and conceal myself where he would not be able to find me, determined to follow in silence.

" He found me in the situation I have before described, and having after a long search, found a spring issuing from a rock, he washed my face and temples, by which means I recovered my senses again. Miserable as I was, a transient gleam of joy ran through my soul on beholding my trusty, affectionate servant ; but gloomy reflections took place of that, and I fear will pervade my soul till death puts a period to my life and miseries together.

" The place in which he found me, afforded no shelter from the fury of a storm, which was collecting, we therefore set out in search for a situation that would, and chance directed us to this cavern. About noon the clouds dispersed, and the weather became serere, my man declared he would endeavor to find the way to town, in order to gain some intelligence of my tutor, if possible, and to procure some provisions for me. Though I ardently wished to know how matters had been conducted since the unhappy affair of the preceding evening, and though we could not exist long without some refreshment, yet it was with reluctance I permitted him to go. A thousand doubts and fears possessed my mind, until he returned, and informed me of his success. On

his arrival in town, it was his intention to go to our inn,
but fear being ever watchful, before he ventured to approach, he took care to have a watchful eye about him,
left he should be discovered, and was no sooner within
fight of the house than he perceived it surrounded by
guards. He retreated with some precipitation, down
a narrow lane, which led to a remote part of the town.
Slackening his pace a little, he accidentally met an old
acquaintance, with whom he had contracted an intimacy when attending my father in his travels. His friend
invited him to partake of a bottle of wine, to which he
complied, and while drinking, they enquired of each
other the particulars of their travels, employment, &c.
They both answered without reserve. " My friend,"
said the other to my man, " I am sorry to find you
are in the service of a person, who if found, will meet
the most rigorous treatment, if not an ignominious
death. The old gentleman, his companion, is now in
a dungeon, as well as the Friar and landlord ; and I
am afraid that will not be the greatest punishment the
Governor will inflict on them, for he is much enraged
against them. I was present at their whole examination, and though there does not appear any cause of
accusation against any but the Friar, they will share the
same punishment."

" My man then requested him to tell every circumstance he knew, which he did in a few words. He
informed him, that an ancient Duenna, who had nursed
Terentia, and had a real affection for her, seeing her set

out towards the Friar's cell, refolved to follow and accompany her home, but on feeing her fo familiarly give
me her hand and enter the wood with me, returned inftantly, and informed the Governor of the difcovery fhe
had made, who immediately ordered his guards to go
to Friar John's cell, and bring every perfon he found
there inftantly before him. The dear creature difclaim-
ed all manner of knowledge or acquaintance with me :
That fhe had met a gentleman on her entering the wood,
fhe confeffed, but denied having any difcourfe with him.
The Friar alfo perfifted in having feen her come alone
to the cell, and that there had been no other perfon
there that evening.

" Notwithftanding all their affeverations of innocence,
the Friar was committed to the dungeon, and my dear
bride to the care of the Duenna, with orders to keep
her clofely confined from the fight of every perfon but
herfelf. " Your horfes," continued his friend, " were
found in the poffeffion of a man, who would not deliver
them to any perfon but fome of the Governor's houfhold : The landlord, and the old gentleman took him
by force and conveyed him to town late laft night,
confined him in a room till this morning, when they
obtained an audience of the Governor, and had
their prifoner examined. His examination developed
the whole affair, for he produced a note in the hand
writing of Terentia, charging him to keep the horfes
fafely, until the bearer or fome other of her father's
domeftics fhould demand them, and not then with-

out her orders in writing. On being afked who delivered the horfes to him, he anfwered he believed it
to be one of the Governor's Eunuch's, and that he was
fure he fhould know him if he could fee him again.
All the Eunuchs were then brought into the prefence of
the governor, and the man inftantly pointed out the
culprit.   He denied the fact pofitively, and bore the
rack a confiderable time before he difclofed the truth.
He confeffed that his miftrefs had given him orders to
watch two gentlemen from the gardens to their lodgings,
to find out whether they travelled on horfeback or not:
That having performed this, he informed her of every
circumftance, and that fhe gave him money and the
note, charging him to go in the night, take the horfes
out of the ftable, and convey them to the place where
they were found.   The Governor ordered him to be
ftrangled immediately.   The man in whofe cuftody the
horfes were found, was feverely fcourged, for not giving
immediate notice to the Governor of thefe proceedings:"
A guard was fent to the inn to fearch for me, with
orders not to return without me ; and my tutor and
the landlord clofely confined, till I fhould be found.

"This was all he could collect at that time, and
being well affured of the fidelity of his friend, informed
him of my concealment, and begged he would affift
him in procuring fome neceffaries for my fupport : This
he complied with, and they parted, having previoufly
agreed to meet the next day at the fame place.

"My man returned in the evening, much fatigued, having carried this matrafs and cover, befides provifions enough for a week's fubfiftence, and a large flafk of wine.

"When I reflected on the concatenation of circumftances by which my late happinefs, and prefent mife-ry was effected, I could not but admire the power of love, which furmounts every difficulty, and maugre confequences, braves every danger to attain its end. It is obvious, that our horfes were taken for no other purpofe than to detain us in St. Marino fome days longer. But to proceed :—

"From the information of my man, refpecting the fidelity of his friend, I began to entertain hopes of yet regaining my dear Terentia, if there was a poffibility of conveying a letter to her. I communicated thefe ideas to my man, which he faid exactly correfponded with his, and added, that but for the fhortnefs of the time, he would have founded his friend on that fubject, but would not fail to try every expedient to procure me the fatisfaction I defired. He met his friend according to appointment and found every thing to his wifh. His friend is in the fervice of an Englifh gentleman, who lodges in a houfe in a back ftreet, the back windows of which overlooks the Governor's private garden, which is immediately attached to the palace.——— His friend further informed him, that he had formed an intimacy with a female domeftic of the Governor's, by whofe means he could be informed of every particular relative to my affairs. He faid, the Duenna attended the young lady as the fhadow the fubftance; but that he did not doubt finding means to convey her a letter, if committed to his charge. My man affured him of an ample reward if he fucceeded; but with all conjured him not to communicate the fecret to his fair enamoratta. He then, with the affiftance of his friend, procured pen, ink and paper; flint, fteel and candles, and returned to me full of the fuccefs of his negociation. I was overjoyed at the profpect of returning happinefs, and embraced him as a brother—indeed he has manifefted the moft unfhaken attachment, and unwearied diligence in foothing my misfortunes, which demands my utmoft regard.

"The next morning I wrote a letter to my dear girl, wherein I defcribed my dreadful fituation—painted the anguifh of my mind on her particular account, and my forrow for the fate of my beloved tutor. I conjured her by the facred ties which united our fouls, to let me know the fituation of affairs there, and gave her a hint of the fidelity of the perfon who forwarded the letter. I fealed and delivered this to my faithful fervant. "Now, fir," faid he, "don't be alarmed, if you fhould not fee me for a day or two, as it is impoffible to hurry this kind of bufinefs, becaufe it depends entirely upon circumftances, and muft be conducted with the greateft caution." He was gone four days and as many tedious nights: I began to look on my ruin as inevitable. I faw already my man ftretched on the rack —faw the guards afcending the mountain, and was feveral times preparing to take the defperate leap, from which you prevented me to day. It was my determination to efcape my enemies by that means, if ever they fhould difcover my retreat.

"At length, however, he arrived with a letter from her dear hand: (Here he read the letter:) He faid his friend bid him tell me, that he had never run fuch a hazzard in his life, as he did in procuring it. He had taken an opportunity of dropping my letter into the walk before her, when her keeper was at fome diftance behind. Terentia, faw it fall, and cafting her eyes upwards and perceiving him, feemed to hefitate; however, fhe picked it up and thruft it haftily into her bofom. Her keeper overtook her prefently and paffed her, and after fome time went into the palace. During her ftay in the houfe he obferved my wife, feated in a fhady fpot, reading the letter, with much apparent emotion. She fuppreffed her agitation, and feemed anxious to fpeak to him; but that was impoffible, as the Duenna juft then returned. The next morning, very early, he pofted himfelf at the window, and though it was but juft day light, fhe was there. She perceived him immediately, and fhowed him a billet which fhe feemed anxious to convey to him. He made a fign to her to throw it down, and retire, giving her to underftand that he would defcend for it, fhe underftood him and immediately complied. He then, by the help of a rope-ladder, which was kept in the houfe

P

in cafe of fire, defcended fpeedily, took up the letter, and returned to his poft; then taking up his ladder he ftood fome minutes, till the dear creature, who had been obferving his motions, returned to the fpot where fhe had left the letter, and perceiving it gone, looked up at him with a glow of fatisfaction on her counte-nance, and retired into the houfe. His friend further faid that he did not conceive it impoffible to deliver her entirely from her confinement, and if I could devife means to convey her out of Italy immediately, he would freely undertake it.

" You fee gentlemen," faid he, " that my worthy tu-tor is condemned to linger out his days in a miferable dungeon, and felf prefervation will not permit me to take any ftep towards effecting his liberation. This thought afflicts me beyond meafure. If he had incur-red his punifhment by any mifconduct of his own, I fhould have been fenfibly afflicted; but the reflection of his being entirely innocent, and of the whole crime being mine, diftracts me, and, I fear, will make fuch an impreffion of grief on my mind, as will never be ef-faced.

" My fervant is now gone with a letter to inform my dear Terentia that I am determined to free myfelf and her quickly, or perifh in the attempt. He is alfo to requeft his friend to affift him in procuring beafts to convey us to Leghorn, where, if we fucceed, I will embark for England immediately. This, gentlemen,

is the sum of my unhappy story, and I think you must
acknowledge my misfortunes to be peculiarly distres-
sing: such as, I hope, you will never experience."

They confessed he had been unfortunate, but ex-
horted him to be cheerful, for that his case, at present,
was by no means desperate ; that he had now reason to
expect that his affairs would take a favourable turn.
They informed him of their intended voyage, and promised him every possible assistance. Just at this instant
the servant arrived.

The servant started at the sight of strangers, and was
going to retire, but his master, perceiving his intention
prevented him, saying, Fear nothing, here are none
but friends: Come forward, how have you sped ?
At that instant Mercutio and George arose, with an
intention to retire ; but Eugenio insisted on their stay
until his servant should have disclosed the result of his
negociation. They acquiesced, and he desired the
servant to inform them, without reserve, of all his
transactions since his departure from thence : He began as follows :—

"I met my friend at the appointed place, who informed me that the Governor of St. Marino intends
paying a visit to the Doge of Venice, in a very short
time : He added, that the lady is not so closely confined as she has been, being now permitted to walk in the
garden alone. He advises you, sir, to remain here

until her father fets out for Venice ; in the mean time,
he promifes to arrange matters fo as to effect the liberation of the lady immediately after the departure of her
father."

He then delivered a letter which, he faid, his friend
had procured from the lady's own hand. Eugenio
feized it, and read it with avidity, then prefenting it to
Mercutio, faid, Behold a flight fpecimen of her mental
accomplifhments, and tell me whether the communication of happinefs appears to be intimately connected
with fuch perfection, or not.

After perufing it attentively, our hero and his friend
could not withhold their affent to his propofition:
They beftowed the greateft encomiums on the amiable
and beloved writer, who, by the fpirit, eafe and ele-
gance with which fhe wrote, would have arrefted the
attention, and extorted the approbation of the moft
furly critic. To the moft ardent vows of eternal fidelity, united with wifhes for her deliverance, fhe added
an intimation of her father's intended journey to Venice, and a minute account of the particular rout he
defigned to take.

Mercutio enjoined Eugenio to make himfelf perfectly eafy, as from the prefent face of his affairs, he
had every reafon to hope they would fhortly terminate
to his entire fatisfaction. George heartily joined in
the admonition, and added, that his houfe and purfe

were at his fervice, together with all the perfonal af-
fiflance in his power. " My beloved friends,". faid
the aftonifhed Eugenio, " how fhail I render you a
proper return for your unparalelled generofity? The
liberality, and extenfive latitude of your offers, when I
reflect on my prefent critical fituation, and the danger
to which you expofe yourfelves in cafe of difcovery,
really amaze me ! Of one thing I am fure—if the whole
of my future life fhould. be devoted entirely to your
fervice it would fall infinitely fhort of a fuitable return." Common humanity, replied, George, is fufficient in this cafe to prompt us to contribute to your relief, therefore we can have no claim on your gratitude ;
for all the good offices we can poffibly perform in behalf of each other will entitle us to no other reward,
than a confcioufnefs of having performed a part of that
duty, which, as men, we owe one to another. If by
any thing in our power, your happinefs is fecured,
we fhall participate with you in the conviction of having acted with propriety ; and the only acceptable return you can make, is your friendfhip, independent of
acknowledgments.

This effectually filenced Eugenio, and George propofed to retire: " In the evening," faid he, " I will
fend a perfon to conduct you and your fervant to my
houfe, which is but a fhort diftance from hence, where
you fhall be properly accommodated, and may remain
in as much privacy as here, till your affairs are brought
to an iffue." Eugenio was about to return an anfwer

full of grateful acknowledgments; but they politely taking leave, and bidding him fear nothing, departed.

As they defcended the mountain, their difcourfe naturally turned on the amazing revolutions of human affairs. " Eugenio," faid George, " was beginning to grow defperate yefterday, and if we had not difcovered his retreat, it is more than probable he would have attempted the regaining his wife by means which, perhaps, might have terminated in his deftruction." " Very likely," replied Mercutio; " the fenfe of his misfortunes had nearly overcome his reafon and fortitude: How often are we prevented, by the interpofition of Divine Providence from the commiffion of that, which, if permitted, would involve us in inevitable ruin! Then how thankful ought we to be to that mighty Being which fpake all things into exiftence, for his merciful condefcenfion in reftraining us from actions which, if committed, his juftice muft have feverely punifhed."

Having regained the foot of the mountain, they were joined by their ladies, who were taking a walk along the fea fhore, the ground between which and the mountain being covered with a delightful verdure, with fine tufts of trees interfperfed, on the boughs of which millions of birds fat finging; the azure concave was beautifully clear to the extremity of the horizon, and every object confpired to render their excurfion agreeable. It was in this delightful fpot that George informed the ladies of the difcovery his friend and he had that morning made. They liftened with aftonifhment and expreffed the utmoft folicitude for the fuccefs of Euge-nio and Terentia. They next confulted on the moft falutary meafures to be employed with regard to their intended journey, and after rejecting feveral propofi-tions, agreed, that preparations fhould be made for a fudden departure, horfes provided, ready to ftart at a minute's warning, and all things packed up ready to lay on them. It was alfo thought requifite that Eugenio and Terentia fhould affume the appearance of fervants, at leaft till their arrival at Florence, in order, by concealing their quality, to prevent difcovery. Thefe preliminaries being agreed to, George inftructed a fervant how to afcend the mountain and to conduct Eugenio down thither in the twilight.

Eugenio arrived attended by his guide and fervant juft as candles were lighting. The reception he met with, reflected the higheft honour on the feelings of his new found friends: He was introduced to the ladies by Mercutio; they received him with marks of the moft profound refpect.

Eugenio was a handfome perfon, perfectly well fhaped and extremely polite; his complexion fair, his features manly; and though his late misfortunes had, in fome meafure, checked his natural vivacity, yet re-turning hope rendered his company very agreeable, which, added to his mental qualifications, fecured him a ftrong prepoffeffion in the affections of his new friends,

who now actually confulted the eafe and fafety of their
gueft more than their own.

After fupper, George informed Eugenio of the
plan which had been adopted, which he highly approved, exprefled much furprize at the promptitude of his
friends to ferye him, and promifed eternal friendfhip in
return.

Early on the following day, Eugenio difpatched his
man with a letter to Terentia, informing her of his fortunate fituation, and of the plan projected by his friends:
He likewife fent a handfome prefent to his agent in
town, requefting at the fame time, his every affiftance
to releafe the lady as foon as the Governor fhould depart, affuring him of an ample reward. The man had
orders to conceal himfelf in town till an anfwer was
procured. George inftantly began to make the neceffary arrangements for the intended journey, in which
Mercutio affifted him. The houfe in which George
refided was ready furnifhed, therefore his moveables
could be eafily packed in portmantaus, which was
immediately done, while our hero and George went in
queft of horfes, to tranfport them whenever they might
be called for. In the mean time, Eugenio's fervant arrived with a letter from Terentia, in fubftance as follows:

" BELOVED EUGENIO,

" My heart vibrates with joy, at hearing the news of
"your prefent fafety, and of your acquifition of fuch

"noble friends as thofe defcribed in your welcome
"epiftle. The perfon who has promoted our correfpon-
"dence is, though a fervant, a perfon of exalted fenti-
"ments, and has formed a plan for my deliverance,
" which, with the affiftance of Heaven, cannot fail:
" Your fervant will acquaint you with the particulars.——
" Three days more will, I truft, reftore me to my
" dear Eugenio; for my father fets out the day after to-
" morrow.—Father John, your tutor and the keeper
" of the prifon have all abfconded—My father is in a vi-
" olent rage on the occafion, and they are purfued with
" avidity: The perfon who forwards our letters gave
" me this information, for all my difcourfe is with my
" nurfe, and fhe informs me of nothing.—Adieu!
" Hope and fear alternately poffefs my foul, till that
" blifsful hour when heaven fhall kindly reftore Euge-
" nio to the arms of his faithful

" TERENTIA."

Eugenio was tranfported beyond meafure on the perufal of this epiftle, and already anticipated the pleafure
of folding his beloved Terentia in his arms. He fubmitted the letter to the perufal of the ladies, who
heartily congratulated him on the apparent profperous
turn of his affairs; and George and Mercutio returning fhortly after, informed them, they had horfes and
every other neceffary accommodation at command on
the fhorteft notice: " And now," faid Mercutio, " banifh anxiety, fince the good old gentleman, your tutor
has made his efcape; three days, I hope, will reftore

your wife, and if fortune favours us, as many weeks
will place you both out of the reach of danger." Thefe.
words infpired Eugenio with new life, and the vifible
change on his countenance indicated a heart elate with
joy.   Agreeably to his appointment with his friend,
Eugenio's fervant went to town the next day, and had
the fatisfaction of feeing the Governor fet out ; and of
hearing that the fcouts who had been fent in purfuit of
the keeper of the prifon, and his fellow travellers, had
returned without having been able to procure the leaft
intelligence of their rout.   It was then concerted between him and his friend, that on the evening of the enfuing. day, he fhould conduct his mafter to the fpot
where he had met Terentia in order to proceed to Friar John's cell, and there wait the arrival of the lady.
His friend informed him that Terentia was to feign a
flight indifpofition fome hours before that appointed for
the intended enterprize, and retire to her clofet on
pretence of trying to compofe herfelf to fleep.   That
her window overlooked the garden, and was not more
than four feet from the ground, fo that fhe might defcend with fafety : In the mean time, he would fix the
abovementioned ladder of ropes to his own window,
with which fhe was well acquainted, where he would
ftand centinel and inftantly on her approach, drop the
ladder, receive her into the window and, throw a
man's long riding cloak over her, conduct her to the
appointed fpot : He added, that his mafter's being out
of town for a few days would greatly facilitate the undertaking.

Having placed every thing in a proper train in town, Eugenio's fervant returned with a billet from the lady, wherein fhe affured him of her perfect willingnefs, and even impatience to accompany him to any part of the globe.

Eugenio communicated thefe welcome tidings to his friends, who partook of his fatisfaction on the occafion. They then concluded, that it would be prudent to fend for the horfes in the afternoon ; to have the baggage laid on as foon as it was dark, then fet forward and travel all night, and, as George knew the whole road perfectly, to halt as feldom as poffible until they fhould arrive in Leghorn.

The next day all hands were bufy in making the neceffary arrangements for their departure : Eugenio, in a ftate of the utmoft anxiety, thought it the longeft of his life ; nor were his friends lefs anxious. At two o'clock, the fervants were difpatched for the beafts ; at five, Eugenio and his man began to afcend the mountain, and our hero and his friends waited their return in calm fufpence, as though fomething fatal hung on the event. The whole hemifphere was involved in darknefs, when Eugenio and his faithful fervant arrived at the place of affignation. After waiting about half an hour, full of hopes and fears, Eugenio was relieved from all his anxiety, by the appearance of her whom he efteemed more than empires : He clafped her in his arms with ectafy, at the fame time exclaiming, "And do I once more embrace my love! Thanks to all-gracious heaven! Such blifs would be cheaply purchafed with an age of toil and fuſpence." Terentia manifeſted her fatisfaction by the moſt tender careffes, and tears of joy.

After the firſt emotions had fubfided, Eugenio turned to her conductor, faying, "And you, my much efteemed friend! How fhall I ever reward your merit as it deferves? You have rendered me a kindnefs which I can never repay. But (pulling out a purfe of gold and prefenting it) accept this trifling teſtimony of my efteem, until an opportunity fhall offer when I may have it in my power to do more juſtice to your worth." He refufed it peremptorily—perfuafions were vain, he would not touch a fingle ducat, and it was with fome difficulty that he was prevailed on to accept a ring which Eugenio forced on his finger, faying, "Wear this, as a token of my friendſhip, till you return to London, when you muſt return it; and I will fupply its place by fomething more worthy of your acceptance."

They then took an affectionate leave of each other and parted. Eugenio's man led the way bearing a very weighty cafket belonging to Terentia: They were a confiderable time defcending the mountain, but arrived fafely at George's juſt as fupper was ferved up. Terentia was received with politenefs and affection; and, after refting herfelf a little, fat down to fupper with them. Preparation was inſtantly made for their departure, Mercutio and George undertook to equip Eugenio, and the ladies difguifed Terentia, who confented to perfonate Ifabella's waiting woman. In the mean time, the fervants faddled the horfes and laid on the baggage, and, after imploring the affiftance and protection of heaven, they mounted and fet forward.

They arrived at Leghorn without meeting with any material occurrence, where they were received with the moft unaffected cordiality by Mr. Wilcox and his amiable fpoufe, who, though fomewhat advanced in years, was poffeffed of the moft perfect good nature, added to a fuperior degree of good fenfe, and a moft pleafing vivacity combined with an elegant form and unacceptionable features.

Mr. Wilcox had two fons, the eldeft commanded a ftout merchant fhip in the Levant trade; the youngeft was factor to his father, in Amfterdam; and two daughters, the youngeft was then in Holland with her brother; and the eldeft was married to George Wright.

The old gentleman had already provided a fhip to tranfport them to Holland, which he had freighted himfelf: He intended to remain in Amfterdam a few weeks, till his fon Robert fhould have difpofed of what merchandize he had on hand, expecting the return of his other fon from the Levant, and then to return to Liverpool with his whole family. They remained but ten days in Leghorn, for George having

informed his father and mother-in-law of the adventure
of Eugenio and Terentia, they judged it the moſt expedient to keep them in diſguiſe while on ſhore, and to
embark as ſoon as convenient. In the mean time Mr.
Wilcox and his ſon-in-law were buſy in ſeeing their effects embarked and ſafely ſtowed on board the ſhip. One
day they found the captain engaged in diſcourſe with a
ſtranger, who ſeemed to preſs earneſtly for ſome
favor: The Captain perceiving Mr. Wilcox, interrupted the ſtranger, ſomewhat haſtily, ſaying, here is
the gentleman of whom I was ſpeaking, if he is willing
to grant your requeſt I have not the leaſt objection.

    " What is your requeſt Sir?" ſaid Mr. Wilcox, in
the moſt unreſerved manner, " I ſhall think myſelf
happy in having it in my power to oblige a gentleman
of your appearance, therefore pray let me hear your
requeſt, and rely on my willingneſs to ſerve you."
" You do me a great deal of honour, Sir," ſaid the
ſtranger, " and I cannot enough admire your frankneſs
and generoſity, in ſo freely tendering me your ſervice.
Not to keep you longer in ſuſpence, I am a native of
England, and have been tranſacting ſome affairs in Italy for a certain nobleman in London: Having lately
received letters from thence preſſing me to return on a
very important affair, I am in haſte to get thither. After having, in vain enquired for a veſſel bound for England, I was informed of this being ſhortly to ſail for
Holland; I therefore made application to the commander, who informs me, that you have already en-

gaged his ship entirely, and that without your consent he could not pretend to take any passengers on board. Now Sir, if you will be kind enough to permit me to sail with you to your destined port, as my affairs are very pressing, I shall esteem it as a favor of the first magnitude, and will comply with every requisite for my passage." " Say no more, sir," said Mr. Wilcox : " You are not only welcome to your passage, but, as I promise myself much satisfaction in your company, I shall make that the only condition." " Your generosity," returned the stranger, " demands all my gratitude, and you may rest assured of my eternal acknowledgment of the obligation." He would have proceeded, but Mr. Wilcox prevented him by informing him, that he intended to embark his family early the next morning, and sail whenever the wind should serve, therefore, advised him, if he had any business to transact on shore, to be as expeditious as possible.

They then politely took leave of each other; Mr. Wilcox and George returned to their friends, and the stranger having no business on shore, remained on board with the Captain.

Three hours before day, our little community arose, and being collected in the common apartment, united in imploring the protection of that God who gave them existence, in their intended voyage. They then began to prepare for embarkation: Eugenio and Terentia put of their menial habits, and appeared in their proper characters. At dawn of day, being all ready, they set forward towards the water-side, where they found the ship's boat waiting. They embarked, and the ship was immediately got under weigh: The canvas being spread to the fresh breeze, they were, in a few hours, wafted out of sight of the city of Leghorn.

Soon after they went on board, Mr. Wilcox enquired for the stranger, and was informed he was not stirring yet. They were all sitting on the quarter deck, congratulating each other on the extreme pleasant weather with which heaven had favoured them in the commencement of their voyage, when the stranger appeared upon deck, and advancing, saluted the whole company in the politest manner. But how shall I paint the astonishment of Eugenio, when in the person of the stranger, he perceived his beloved tutor? He sprang forward, and eagerly embracing him, exclaimed aloud, " Do I behold, once more, my honoured, my much loved master, friend and companion, alive and at his liberty." Then falling on his knees, earnestly intreated him to pardon the folly of his youth, which had nearly involved them both in irretreivable ruin.

" Rise my child," said his tutor, with a countenance that discovered the goodness of his soul, " and may heaven pardon every inadvertency of your future life as freely as I do this first: As to the inconveniencies I may have met with since our seperation, they were of no consideration with me, when compared with the

anxiety I experienced on your particular account, left
you ſhould be diſcovered. After all I am happy in the
reflection of having your company to Englanl; and of
having in my power then to preſent you ſafe to your
noble parents."

"My dear ſir," replied the youth, "your generoſity, from our firſt interview, has been familiar to me;
but in this particular inſtance manifeſts itſelf in ſo ſuper-
lative degree, that it leaves me a bankrupt, by conferring an obligation too vaſt for me ever to acquit myſelf of." He then took Terentia by the hand, and
preſented her to his tutor, ſaying, "behold, dear ſir
the innocent, beloved cauſe of our late troubles; and
ſeal my pardon by admitting her to a ſhare of your
eſteem." The old gentleman prevented her from kneel-
ing, by catching her in his arms, as ſhe was taking
that poſture: He aſſured her of his warmeſt friendſhip,
adding, that he had never imputed the leaſt part of his
late troubles to her intention. She declared her ſa-
tisfaction in being honoured with the regard of ſo worthy a perſon; and promiſed to reſpect him as one of
her beſt friends. Breakfaſt interrupted the converſation for ſome time. When over, Mr. Savigny, Eugenio's tutor, requeſted of his pupil the particulars of
his adventures ſince they parted in St. Marino. Eugenio accordingly related, in the moſt connect manner,
every circumſtance, as it has been communicated to
the reader already: Painting, in the moſt ſtriking colours the favours he had experienced at the hands of

Q 2

his new friends. "Mr. Savigny liftened attentively to every part of his narrative, not without emotion, and when it was ended, remarked, that the hand of Providence had been vifibly exerted in favour of them both; adding, that nothing fhort of a complete affiance in the protection of the Supreme Being, could have encouraged him even to hope for an efcape from the horrid dungeon in which he, had been confined. The whole company then requefted a fimilar favour of Mr. Savigny.

"My adventures," faid he, "in fo fhort a fpace, cannot be fuppofed to have been many or important; and though interefting to me, will afford neither pleasure nor amufemement to the company prefent: Yet, it would argue the moft unpardonable ingratitude in me, to refufe fo flight a gratification to perfons who have fo generoufly contributed to my prefent happinefs, and that of my pupil, in fo extenfive a latitude. The day I parted with you," turning to Eugenio, "You know I fet out in company with our hoft, in order, if poffible, to recover our horfes. The perfon in whofe poffeffion we found them, refufed to deliver them without a written order from the Governor or fome of his houfhold: We were much furprized at this repulfe, and demanded his reafons. He anfwered, that they were delivered to him by one of the Governor's Eunuchs, who charged him to keep them fafely, feed them well, and that he fhould be amply rewarded; and moreover delivered him a billet from

the Governor's daughter :" (Here Terentia withdrew
with Isabella,) " which contained peremptory orders
not to deliver the horses to any person without the
aforementioned order.

" This answer did but involve me in greater perplexity, for, what business the Governor of St. Marino
could have with our horses, or how he came by them,
was to me, an inexplicable mystery. I told him the
horses were mine, that I suspected he wished to im-
pose on me ; that the story he had vamped up appeared
to me a fiction, and the note a forgery. I told him
further, that if he would deliver up the horses immediately, I should give myself no further trouble ; if not,
that I would make immediate application to the Governor, and have him severly punished for his obstinacy.

" Finding that all I said had no effect, I left him,
and with my landlord, returned to St. Marino, and
soon obtained an audience with his Excellency : This
was the next day about ten o'clock. After having
made my complaint, he promised me ample satisfaction and instantly dispatched an officer and twelve men
with orders to bring the delinquent before him immediately. He was brought there in a few hours, when
the Governor proceeded to interrogate him : He immediately produced the billet. The Governor having
perused it, asked who delivered him the horses ? Antonio, replied the prisoner. He then asked him if

Antonio had affigned any reafon for bringing them to him ; he anfwered in the negative.

"The Eunuch was fent for, and examined. He trembled exceedingly, his tongue faltered, and his anfwers were fhort, broken and ambiguous. The Governor commanded him to the torture——He confeffed the whole, corroborated what the prifoner had faid, and completely unravelled the whole affair. The Governor, having obtained all the information the unfortunate Eunuch could give, ordered him to be ftrangled : My feelings revolted at this piece of cruelty, and I could not refrain foliciting pardon for the trembling victim ; but in vain : He flew into a violent rage and began to interrogate the landlord and me concerning you, at which we were aftonifhed, not doubting but you was ftill at our lodgings.

"In vain we affured him we had neither feen nor heard from you fince we had fet out in fearch of the horfes : He infifted our anfwers were all evafions ; that we had all confpired together to rob him of his daughter, and perhaps his life. One mifcreant, faid he, has atoned for his crimes by death, and, if that heretic, meaning you, is not fpeedily difcovered, you may reft affured of a fimilar fate : Drag them away, faid he to the keeper of the prifon, confine them clofely ; if you fuffer them to efcape, your life fhall pay the forfeit.

" Accordingly we were conveyed to the common prifon, where we were confined in a moft horrid dungeon,
denied the benefit of light or air, and in continual expectation of being ftrangled or broke on the wheel.
The fecond day of our imprifonment, the landlord was
releafed, in order (as the goaler has fince informed
me) to detect, if poffible, you or your fervant, who
it was fuppofed, would be keeping a look out for me.
Dreary as my habitation, and gloomy as my future
profpect was, my ardent prayer to heaven was, that
I might be permitted to endure the utmoft vengeance
of the Governor, rather then you fhould be difcovered.

" One night, as I lay, enveloped in the moft gloomy
darknefs, ruminating on my unhappy fituation, and
praying for your fafety, I thought I heard fomebody
difcourfing in a very low key. I raifed my head and
liftened very attentively.—I foon perceived, through a
very fmall crevice, the Goaler and a perfon in a cano-
nical habit (who afterwards proved to be the Friar
who married you) in clofe converfation together:
They were forming a plan for abandoning the prifon
the enfuing night, and to poft away to the dominions
of Spain with all poffible fpeed.

" Hopelefs as my fituation was, a ray of hope darted
through my foul with the idea of converting the difcovery to my own advantage. A variety of refolutions
prefented themfelves, to my diftracted imagination,
between that time and the dawning of the day. At all

events, I resolved to hint the matter to the Goaler, let him know I had discovered their whole plan, and finally, request a participation in their adventure: I was encouraged to this measure by an idea that he would never (if he could help it) return to Italy, consequently would be regardless of the consequences which might attend his elopement : He might also be apprehensive of my discovering their rout.

" I slept very little that night, and that little was interrupted by dreams, by no means agreeable, and when I awoke, my heart palpitated violently; my whole frame was much agitated, tho' unconscious of any crime, either committed or meditated.

" Morning, if the appearance of the Goaler may be termed so ; for light never intruded my apartment, at length dispelled the perturbation of my mind ; my keeper appeared more civil than ordinary; which I interpreted as a good omen. He presented my usual modicum of food—I received it with a heavy sigh, exclaiming at the same time, When Oh Lord ! shall I be released from this racking situation ?—Thrice happy, said I, turning to the keeper, are you my friend, in the enjoyment of that liberty, of which I am unjustly deprived ! How happy should I be now, could I be permitted to breathe, once more the fresh air ! Once more enjoy the light of heaven!—But alas ! I am, I fear, if not to suffer an ignominious death, doomed to linger out the remainder of my days in this loathfome den, excluded from the fociety of men, with a mind tortured with the moft racking anxiety, without having committed even the fhadow of a crime.

" I really commiferate your diftrefs, but you know, faid he, the nature of my employment will not admit of my contributing to the alleviation of it.   Oh yes, anfwered I, it is in your power to refcue me from the impending mifchief which awaits me.   If you intended to remain here, I fhould not put your fidelity to the trial.   He appeared much embarraffed.   But be not offended nor furprized, when I inform you, that your intentions are well known to me : I overheard every word that paft between you and the reverend father laft night ;. and all I requeft in confequence is, that you will admit me a partner in your intended enterprize.

" His countenance changed, and he was about to reply; but I prevented him, by faying, only reflect, my dear friend, on the confequences refulting from your clopement : You fee how rigoroufly I am already treated, without any caufe, and is it not more than probable that when the Governor is informed of the ftep you have taken, he will wreak his whole vengeance on me ?—I fee humanity in your countenance—I am convinced you have not a wifh to be acceffary to my death, which will inevitably follow your departure. Oh confider this, my dear friend, faid I, taking his hand, you are fenfible my prefent confinement is unmerited ; therefore, let me take my lot with you this

night, let what will befal me, I will be your everlaſt-
ing friend.—Here I pauſed.   Your requeſt ſhall be
granted, ſaid he, I am going to Father John now ;
and will return to you ſhortly ; in the mean time,
make yourſelf eaſy : If we ſucceed, this night you
ſhall be at your liberty ; if not, inevitable ruin attends
us all.

" He left me, and I muſt confeſs I wronged him ;
for I was doubtful of his integrity : He returned, however, according to his promiſe, and informed me, that
he had conſulted with the Holy father ; that he was
well ſatisfied for me to accompany them to ſome diſtance from the town ; but that then I muſt ſhift for
myſelf.——I will, continued he, furniſh you with a
horſe of my own, which you may diſpoſe of as you
think proper, and twenty ducats to bear your ex-
pences till you are out of danger.   With theſe
words he preſented me with this purſe, (ſhowing
it) containing the aforeſaid ſum and this dagger :
You may, perhaps, find this your beſt friend, ſaid
he.   Farewell—hold yourſelf in readineſs——doubt
nothing.

END OF VOLUME FIRST.

www.ingramcontent.com/pod-product-compliance
Lightning Source LLC
Chambersburg PA
CBHW030555040726
47497CB00008B/2742